MEMORY & DESIRE

MEMORY & DESIRE

LUISA SMITH

iUniverse, Inc.
New York   Bloomington

MEMORY AND DESIRE

iUniverse books may be ordered through booksellers or by contacting:

iUniverse
1663 Liberty Drive
Bloomington, IN 47403
www.iuniverse.com
1-800-Authors (1-800-288-4677)

Because of the dynamic nature of the Internet, any Web addresses or links contained in this book may have changed since publication and may no longer be valid. The views expressed in this work are solely those of the author and do not necessarily reflect the views of the publisher, and the publisher hereby disclaims any responsibility for them.

ISBN: 978-1-4502-3684-3 (sc)
ISBN: 978-1-4502-3891-5 (ebk)

Printed in the United States of America

iUniverse rev. date: 06/18/2010

CHAPTER ONE

Daria's father, Ivan Khazmanov, had the kind of charisma that could both attract and repel. He was a brash, brazen man whose charm lay in his seeming simplicity, a persona he projected through a cultivated buffoonery. On first meeting, he'd pull a man to him and declare, "I'm Russian. You know this? In Russia men kiss men." Or, he'd bluster, "I'm strong like bull," in imitation of Popeye, his favorite cartoon character.

Daria's first inkling of the truth about her father came with her reading of <u>In Innocent Blood</u>, recommended by Dr. Freid. "Why this cheap thriller?" she protested. When obscure recollections began to surface, she blurted, "Sounds like we're talking about incest."

"Tell me that's not it," she demanded.

A week later she wrote the doctor a note: "I will no longer be requiring your services." Thus ending their nine year relationship. She chose poetry readings instead, leaving home evenings warmed by Jake's and Hannah's embraces. But turning onto the West Side Highway, eyeing, the dark, secret waters of the East River, she became pensive, gloomy.

In the near empty auditorium, later, where she sat alone listening to solitary authors read from an immense stage, she felt adrift. Engulfed in fog. The words of the poems seemed to evaporate before they reached her, and she left each reading flooded by vaguely disturbing images.

Back on the highway, braving the winter dark, she kept checking the rear view mirror. The black river, the swollen clouds, the sleek asphalt dotted with stark light -- in everything she sensed a menace. And each week, as she drove to and from the city, the enigma which had always hung like a dim curtain over her life seemed to become an ever more palpable presence.

Birds inundated her dreams. Hundreds of them crowded her apartment, or she found them in her school letterbox, their wings broken, yet able to reach the floor and totter about.

∾

For years she'd stayed clear of her father, but since her re-marriage he'd plied them with gifts. First, a new countertop, to which Jake agreed over her opposition.

"What're you doing here?" she shouted one day when she found Ivan working in her kitchen.

"Jake gave me the key. Don't you remember?" he said, grinning.

When he next offered them a chandelier, Daria warned, "Don't take it."

"Why not?" Jake said, to which she had no reply

Next came a lithograph -- a black and white drawing of an

Orthodox Jewish bride and groom standing under the *chupa* surrounded by traditionally garbed on lookers. "It's beautiful," Jake said and she had to agree. But the sight of this tender scene in her father's rough hands rattled her. He was up to something, she knew, trying to con his way back into her heart.

Still, at Jake's insistence Daria accepted Ivan's gifts and even threw him a birthday party. The family came together that evening in high spirits -- Jake and Daria because they'd moved into a new apartment, her sister Mimi because she was expecting, Ivan and Bronya because they were being feted. Seated together in the living room, they sang and clapped as Hannah danced with her little cousin, Mitch, while Ivan, his blue eyes aglow, laughed raucously.

Eager to capture this scene of domestic happiness, Daria grabbed the camera. But when she stood peering at her father lounging in her leather armchair, a disbelieving joy suffusing his coarse features, she felt a jolt. An alarm. And she wondered all at once what in the world she was doing. As if she were waking from a spell.

∽

The next day she called Dr. Freid. Would he take her back? But he directed her, instead, to Dr. Agnes Pearle, whose voice on the phone touched her like a caress.

In the therapist's office startling dreams flooded her mind: *She is two people at once, a social worker and a stony faced pregnant girl perched on a fence. Aware of the girl's seduction by a cult leader, the social worker urges the girl to speak. But to no avail.*

A child in a dress is seated on a bleacher, holding cotton candy. A woman seated below catches sight of the girl's naked, semen filled vagina.

Memories followed. *She is eight year old, waking half naked in the woods, her crumpled underwear nearby, a stabbing pain in her abdomen.*

She is a girl sobbing in bed as some strange, panting man presses himself against her back, pushing a knife into her bowels.

She is a teenager depositing her soul into a drawer as footsteps approach her bedroom door. Her disembodied head watches from the ceiling as an assailant smothers her in her bed.

As remembrances poured from her, Daria marveled at her long state of oblivion, at her mind's ability to have retained what it had for so long forgotten. But the more she recalled, the more she felt unhinged. Hallucinatory. And reality became a kind of high wire from which she was at every moment in danger of falling.

The past burned bright but seemed disconnected from the present. The father she knew today, she told herself, was not the predator of yesterday. Yet, she began to observe him more closely, to glance at him surreptitiously, to make dark, insidious connections from which she shrank. But what harm could her aging father do her now, she reasoned. What good could possibly come from bringing up the past?

No, she told herself; for the sake of the children she would remain silent.

∽∾

Ivan began to complain of strange ailments. He had pains in his legs; his gait stiffened. His body temperature rose and fell. His sinuses became swelled. Was he suffering from rheumatism? A recurrence of the malaria he'd contracted during the war? A bacterial infection? The doctors, Bronya complained in her pungent Yiddish, "know nothing and are worth nothing."

∽∾∾

At the birth of Mimi's son Daria embarked on the short drive to her sister's house in an agitated state. She'd not seen her parents in months and dreaded meeting them now. In the car, with Hannah keeping up a constant chatter beside her, she lost her way, mistakenly entered the Parkway and was stuck in traffic. When she arrived, the house was filled with strangers. But no Mimi. While Hannah searched for her little cousin, Daria looked around the noisy, packed living room feeling dislocated. Bewildered.

Moments later, she spotted Bronya in the living room surrounded by a small group. Dressed in a mauve, fitted suit flattering to her short, stout figure, her bouffant, peroxide hair freshly styled, her angular cheeks rouged and her thin lips a glossy red, she looked, Daria thought, startlingly vivacious. Absorbed in conversation, she was gesticulating with both hands, her usually dour expression so animated as to make her almost unrecognizable. Daria stared at her mother from a distance, waiting to be noticed. But Bronya's gaze remained riveted on her audience. As if she were on stage.

Disheartened, Daria turned away and noticed her father. Seated on the edge of the crowded sofa, he looked gloomy, distracted. Stirred by her old pity for him, she strode across the room. "What's the matter?" she said, squeezing in beside him. "You look terrible."

He was staring into space and seemed not to notice her. "Don't you worry yourself about me. Your father is strong like bull. I outlived the doctors who wanted to cut off my leg in Germany, I'll outlive the doctors here. I'll outlive them all," he shouted above the din, his gaze vacant.

Daria jumped up, unnerved by Ivan's remoteness, his severity. If she left now, she thought, no one would notice. But she went in search of her sister. "Come in," Mimi said, when Daria knocked on her bedroom door.

"So there you are," Daria exclaimed, seeing Mimi seated in bed holding the baby.

"And there *you* are," she retorted with a glower.

Daria stepped back. "What do you mean?" she faltered.

"Where were you?" Mimi cried. "You were supposed to be the godmother at the bris and you missed the whole thing."

"Oh," Daria mumbled. "I got stuck on the Parkway." She would've said more but Mimi's scowl drove her from the room. She wandered around, besieged by questions. What did being a godmother at a bris mean? Who were these people in Mimi's home? When had her sister become an observant Jew? What was the meaning of her hostility?

Catching her mother's eye later, Daria joined her little circle of "landsmen" (people from her home town in Poland). "Did you meet my daughter and granddaughter," Bronya gloated, and Daria shivered with momentary pleasure. When eleven year old Hannah spoke up boldly to the landsmen -- people who'd survived so much they scoffed at all those who'd, "seen nothing and knew nothing," she beamed.

But she left her sister's house that afternoon feeling distracted. Disoriented. Her father's stunned, pitiful expression filled her with remorse. How could the ailing, distracted man she'd just seen be the perpetrator of her memories, she thought. Yet, wasn't it odd that Ivan's symptoms had flared up just as she was seeing him anew -- as if, she thought, he sensed her suspicions of him.

∽⌣∾

Nevertheless, memories of childhood still seemed remote, containable, severed from the present. But recollections of her teenage marriage began to unnerve her. "Make believe it never happened," her parents had advised when the union ended. And at nineteen that had seemed possible to do. Now, old images began to re-surface -- her father parked outside her apartment mornings or waiting for her in his car near the college campus, offering her rides. "Leave the bum already. What do you need him for now?" he'd urged after her miscarriage. But she'd only stiffen, retreat into silence.

One night he'd appeared alone at her front door. "What're you doing here?" she'd snapped at his shadowy figure in the dim hallway.

"Can't a father visit a daughter?" he'd mocked and she had no choice but to let him in. "Does he ever come home that husband of yours? Do you ever see him? Why do you always sit here by yourself?" he'd heckled over coffee. Seated across from him at the kitchen table, she'd broken down, then, put her head in her arms and wept.

That was the night she'd returned to her parents' house for good. But why had she agreed, finally, to leave the apartment? What had happened immediately after the weeping? When had she gotten into her father's car? To these questions she had no answers.

Bit by bit, however, the lost memories began to emerge. Ivan catching her in his embrace. His unshaven cheek rubbing against her face. The sound of his groans, "I love you. Don't you know how much I love you?" Her struggle to break free. Then -- the deep, familiar sinking into darkness.

She recalled waking later in the back seat of her father's car, indistinct shouts echoing in the distance, an image of scattered clothing in her mind's eye, her thoughts blurry, remote, as if she'd been drugged.

As the truth of that night dawned on her, Daria began to grasp the ineluctable link between the past and the present – to understand that she could no more disconnect the father of today from the assailant of yesterday than she could cut herself off from her own history. Still, her hold on those years was tenuous. Images flitted like ghosts in and out of her memory. Had the assault in her apartment been the last time, she wondered now. Had Ivan ever accosted her again?

Driving to work one morning she visualized a curtain lifting suddenly to a long forgotten scene. She was seated at her desk in her old bedroom, while the TV blared downstairs. "I'll be at the neighbors," she'd heard her mother shout. And as the front door slammed, she felt an alarm, a shock. How could she leave me alone with him, she recalled thinking.

Suddenly, the TV voices stopped and she heard footsteps on the stairs. Frozen, she stood listening, her heart thudding at his approach. Then he was at her door – a man -- a stranger -- yet utterly familiar. She saw him in a dream, coming toward her. "No! I don't want to," she shouted. And in one hallucinatory moment, she lifted a chair, swung it in the air and threatened to strike her father.

"No?" he said with a shrug, and in a moment, he was gone. As if the episode were inconsequential.

But coming down the stairs later, Daria caught the fear in his eyes, saw him cowering before her. And she understood she'd battled her father for the last time.

These scenes returned to her now with a visceral power. Once more she was the girl who'd stood at her bedroom door listening to approaching footsteps. Once again she felt herself step out of her body as she threatened to brain her father.

For days she relived this final struggle: hearing the sound of Ivan's approach. Feeling her agitation at the sight of him at her door, and the throbbing of every nerve as she swung that chair toward his head. In those few moments, she realized, she'd been in full possession of the truth. Had been aware from the instant she'd heard the front door slam behind her mother that he would come. And she'd known precisely what he was after.

Why, then, had she remained silent? Why hadn't she shouted the truth? Had the knowledge which had compelled her to lift the chair vanished the moment she brought it down? Was the mind capable of keeping secrets from itself?

"You promised not to come into my room anymore!" she recalled raging at Ivan at age sixteen, the memory as startling as if she'd just stepped into another's skin. Had she actually conversed, then, with her father about his assaults, she wondered. And had she, on some level, even cooperated, she thought with horror.

As other, similar recollections surfaced she began to grasp the anomaly of a dual consciousness, of her having become, in fact, two people at once. But while the past became ever more transparent, the road ahead appeared increasingly hazardous.

CHAPTER TWO

Their new suburban house, Daria knew, was the realization of her parents' own unfulfilled immigrant dream. While most of Bronya and Ivan's refugee friends had become prosperous through entrepreneurship, Ivan, with his minimal education and lack of business skills ("I don't have a head for business," he'd say of himself), barely rose above the laboring class. And while he and Bronya had managed to buy a modest, attached home in Queens, their income never approximated that of Bronya's landsmen or even that of her sister -- a life long source of bitterness for her.

As an adolescent Daria would often hear about the grand houses on Long Island where Ivan worked in construction. And he'd occasionally take the family on tours of these manicured neighborhoods beyond their reach. In rebellion against her parents' materialism, Daria had never aspired to affluence, and yet -- ironically, in middle age, she found herself living the life her parents had always craved.

Caught between joy and despair, she lived now in a constant state of suspense. Memories of her father's nighttime incursions into her bedroom left her stunned. Immobilized. But on moving day, when she looked out at the tree lined streets of her new suburban world, the past seemed remote. Irrelevant. With so much good fortune she felt euphoric. Resolute. And she fell in love with everything. The comfortable house. The spacious yard. The affluent neighborhood. These, she told herself, are tangible. The rest -- mere ghosts and shadows. Her only dilemma, she thought, was deciding how to live with her all too real parents of today.

She tried to keep them at bay, postponed inviting them to the new home, and when she did, it was not for the expected Sunday lunch but for a week day evening coffee.

"At night? You want us to come at night?" Bronya complained.

꽁

On the evening her parents were due to arrive, the phone rang a half hour before the appointed time. "Daria?" she heard her mother shout at the other end.

"What happened?" she asked.

"He had an accident."

"An accident?"

"Yes. And it's your fault!"

"My fault?"

"Yes. You told us to come at night. You know he can't see so good at night," Bronya screamed.

Ivan's accident turned out to be minor. But shaken, he'd returned home.

Daria next invited her parents to Hannah's school concert, an afternoon which began with a jolt. She was in the kitchen, gazing out the window, a dish towel in hand, when she caught sight of a man standing in the yard with his back turned. A trespasser, she thought in alarm, then realized with a shock she was looking at her father. He was staring at her through the window, smiling triumphantly, his mouth open, his rough face flushed with pleasure -- as if he'd just outsmarted her.

Daria stood staring at him, her heart clamoring, when the door bell rang. "What in the world is he doing?" she asked Bronya in greeting.

"Do I know? He's a mishuganeh," (lunatic), Bronya said, stepping inside.

Ivan appeared just as Daria was closing the door. Bounding into the living room, he declared, "Not bad. Not bad," and proceeded to roam the house. "Bronya, come up here," he shouted. "You gotta see this." Daria, Ivan and Bronya trudged up the stairs. "You're O.K.," Ivan declared when they all stood together in the bedroom. "In my book you're A one O.K.," he went on, thumping Jake on the back, his face fever red.

"Hannah. Let's go," Daria called in agitation.

"Hello, my goldeneh kiind," (golden child) Daria heard Bronya say as she ran down to the garage.

Her hands shook as she started the car. "Hey. What're you doing?" Jake shouted while she backed into the driveway. But it was too late. She'd shattered the side view mirror. "What the hell's going on?" Jake said.

"Oh, I don't know," she moaned. "You take the wheel."

In the car Hannah conversed with her grandparents. "It's a good thing the other kids will be drowning me out, grandma," she said. "My violin playing is terrible."

"I'm sure everything you do is wonderful, my goldeneh kiind," Bronya said.

The sky that day shone a lustrous blue and as the family traversed the lush green high school campus Daria was dazzled by her good fortune. She came into the auditorium beaming --

at the kids on stage, the well dressed audience streaming in and Hannah dressed in satin and velvet, waving to her grandparents from a distance.

Yet, something in her shuddered. She couldn't see her father but she could sense him -- as if his hectic presence filled the hall. At intervals she'd catch sight of him leaned forward, looking past his wife, past Jake, his head of now mostly white hair turned toward her. He was trying to draw her attention to him, she knew, hoping she'd return his too bright gaze, trying to reassert his loony sense of their intimacy. But Daria kept her eyes rigidly averted.

When they filed out of the auditorium later she ran ahead and afterwards, with everyone's attention focused on Hannah, was easily able to avoid her father, so that, all in all, their charade of a happy family group, she thought, had gone off well. The five of them spilled out onto the school lawn full of smiles and chatter -- Hannah calling out greetings to passing classmates as they headed toward the parking lot.

Back in the car they kept up the convivial mood. Bronya was full of praises. "I wish I could go to such a wonderful school. I had to leave school at fourteen in Poland. Did you know this mameleh?" she said wistfully, while Ivan remained uncharacteristically silent. Daria could see him from the rear view mirror, staring wide eyed at his surroundings. If their months of separation had affected him at all, nothing in his demeanor betrayed his distress. His health had rallied in recent weeks and he bounded out of the car with marked vigor. For a moment, he stood beside his wife in the driveway, his expression eager and beaming.

"Nu?" Bronya said.

"The three of us are going out for pizza. You want to come?" Daria mumbled, looking away from her mother's expectant expression.

"No.We do not want pizza," Bronya sneered.

Ivan stood dumbfounded. Daria averted her gaze, the aborted family scenario flickering in her mind's eye -- the five of them seated around the large kitchen table laden with the usual breads, cheeses and meats, the walls resounding with their frenzied laughter and over heated chatter. She glanced from one parent to the other.

Bronya was already heading toward the car but Ivan remained rooted, as if unwilling to relinquish hope. In his stunned expression Daria read his struggle with disappointment, bewilderment, resignation. For a moment they faced one another -- like two combatants. And though Daria stood only two feet from him she felt she was seeing her father from a distance. She noticed his eyes -- bloodshot and speckled, giving him a diseased look that belied his air of health.

"Well," he said with a low moan, his mouth trembling. "Don't be a stranger." He extended his arms. But Daria quickly crossed the space between them, brushed her father's dry cheek with her lips and avoided his embrace. "Bye," she called and turned abruptly away. Never to see him again.

It hadn't occurred to her, Daria reflected years later, that her father might die. At sixty-two he'd appeared to be his old self, talking on the telephone in honeyed tones, repulsing questions about his health with a gruff, "Don't you worry yourself about me."

But just as Daria was about to banish her father from the upper regions of her mind the issue of child sexual abuse became widely aired, and she began to question her own secretiveness, especially in regard to Hannah, who at thirteen was old enough for truth. But how to tell her?

She knew that there were women like herself who came together, but she shuddered at the prospect of joining them, imagining unsavory people meeting in seedy surroundings. The reality, however, turned out to be altogether different.

The group she found met in an affluent town forty minutes from home. Here was an imposing clock tower, small shops, lavish foliage, stately homes. The house she entered was a large white Colonial set back on a quiet, tree lined street. She rang the bell, waited and let herself into an elegantly furnished foyer. Examining the décor she thought she might've wandered into the wrong place when a stylishly dressed woman in her fifties came rushing toward her. "Come in. Come in," she said in a smoker's voice, a smile radiating from her worn, expertly made up face. Daria followed her into a richly furnished parlor: brocade drapes, deep pile sofas, plush carpet. For a moment, Daria took it all in. Then she perused the women. About fifteen of them were seated in a circle, their well groomed appearance more suggestive of a Hadassah group than victims of rape.

They called themselves incest survivors, a term Daria had never before heard but which instantly conferred on her an odd sense of inclusion. And as she observed the group from her comfortable armchair in this pleasant, well appointed room, any compunction she'd felt about being among them melted away. They were led by Jill, a social worker who distributed pertinent articles about which a discussion followed. Daria sat mesmerized -- hardly able to believe that these attractive, articulate women shared her history.

In the months ahead she learned that these were mostly tough, straight forward people with jobs, families, accomplishments.

How, she thought, had they done it? And how, she wondered for the first time, had she herself not only survived but thrived.

From early on, she realized, she'd held to her own principles, her mind curiously detached from daily brutalities -- her willed naiveté becoming her strength.

But what of the present, she asked herself. Was she to cower forever in silence? Keep up an untenable pretence all her life? The more she deliberated, however, the more irresolute she felt.

This state of uncertainty ended abruptly. Driving home from Dr. Pearle's one day, her mind in an uproar, she felt all at once that she must speak, must discharge the toxic memories that threatened to unhinge her. Spotting a phone booth, she pulled up, ran inside, and with a trembling hand impulsively dialed her sister's number. At the sound of Mimi's "hello," she instantly blurted the damning words, "I had sex with my father," and, as if on cue, they both broke into sobs, Mimi's wails bordering on hysteria.

Later, Daria thought she recalled Mimi having exclaimed, "I knew it." And she was gratified. But Mimi's frenzy had caught her off guard. "What am I supposed to do now? How can I look them in the face?" she'd shrieked, as if she were coming unglued.

Alarmed by her sister's agitation, Daria wondered if she couldn't have made her incendiary revelation by degrees. Her own break through, she realized, had been gradual. Cushioned. She'd had years in which to inure herself against the shock. Now she pondered what she might've done differently. Spoken more softly, found less inflaming words, chosen a better moment? But the more she questioned herself, the more she kept reaching the same conclusion: that she could no more have mitigated the sting of her message than she could have undone the past. And now that the truth was out, she felt relieved, little suspecting the ills she'd unloosed.

CHAPTER THREE

Mimi's shrieks over the wires that evening were like the high pitched caterwauling of scared birds before an approaching cataclysm. Seated in her small study, the phone to her ear, Daria imagined the wood paneled walls swaying, as if she were stranded on a stormy sea. My god, she thought, frightened by the tempest she'd unleashed.

"Tell me what to do now?" Mimi screamed.

And Daria, shaken by her sister's violence could only repeat, "Do nothing. At least not till we can talk face to face."

The next afternoon Daria stood at her sister's door in a state of hectic but not unpleasant agitation. Despite Mimi's ravings of the previous day, Daria did not doubt that they would come in the end to an empathetic understanding. All day her mind had buzzed with anticipated scenarios. She and Mimi embracing, weeping, condoling as they used to when they were children. She imagined their passionate exchange -- the years of baffled anguish stripped, finally, of their mystery.

Though Mimi greeted her with puffy eyes that day, she seemed otherwise composed. Hearing the children's' shouts in the background, Daria stepped cautiously inside. With the two boys on hand, the sisters only glanced at one another, an exchange from which Daria took heart. Mimi's look seemed heartfelt, full of promise. The kids settled at their play, the two of them sat down to tea.

"How're you holding up?" Daria began and before long they were, indeed, embracing. But, once again, Mimi could not speak for weeping, emitting deep strangled sobs as she lay limp against her sister's shoulder. For over an hour, interspersed with interruptions from the kids, Mimi kept up a tear soaked lamentation while Daria patted and reassured her. They'd both be better off in the long run, she said. Truth would bring them clarity, freedom. "Get help," she urged. "Take time to think things through." Together they'd figure out how to deal with their parents. "You can count on me," Daria said before leaving. "I'm here for you." Embracing at the door, they parted friends.

Daria left her sister that day feeling both elated and distressed. At long last she and Mimi had voiced the unspeakable -- given a name to the family torment, and after years of chill they'd re-established their early intimacy. Still, Daria thought with some resentment, though Mimi had wept, she'd grieved only for herself -- as if it were she who'd been the victim. Had Ivan, in fact, molested them both, Daria wondered.

Yet, at bottom, she felt hopeful. Her sister had been restored to her. Together, what could they not face, what not overcome, she thought, impatient for their next contact.

It came days later in the form of an envelope addressed

in Mimi's sprawling handwriting delivered to her front door. Surprised, Daria tore into it, expecting a friendly letter. Instead, every word of the five page missive came at her like a blow. She read it with increasing panic, looked up and felt the room spin. Startled into disbelief she read it through again:

"I have thought a lot about the way you called me and dumped your garbage in my lap. The way you told me stuff I didn't need to hear -- and I've decided that whether or not what you've said is true the fact is, you've behaved in a very hostile and destructive way toward me. The fact is that whenever you come back into my life you create havoc for me. I see you as dangerous to my well being. I do not want to hear anymore about what you have uncovered in therapy. Tell it to her! Not to me!"

The letter went on and on in this vein, closing with: "I don't want your kind of relationship. I am locking the door behind me now."

Daria looked up with unseeing eyes, the floor swaying beneath her feet. "No," she thought in a panic, ran to her desk and tossed the pages in a drawer, as if she could thereby rid herself of their content. In the coming days she lived in a kind of stupor, her mind bogged down by oppressive recollections as she tried to account for her sister's startling malice. When another letter arrived days later her spirits rose. An apology, she thought, spotting the envelope at her front door. But no, astonishingly, she found a brief, endearing note ostensibly written by her three year old nephew, Mitch, to Hannah. She ran to the phone, dialed Mimi's number, discharged a volley of frenzied shouts and, shaking with fury, slammed the receiver.

∽✠∾

For weeks afterwards she was weighed down by torpor. Mornings and afternoons the sky seemed bleak and the clogged roadways devoid of humans. Stunned by the choices she'd been dealt: to either perpetuate the family lie or live as an outcast, she wondered if life would have nothing more to offer.

Increasingly, dealing with her parents was like chewing on her own bile. "When're we going to see you already?' her mother asked with peevish insistence.

And, Ivan, in the rare instances when he answered the phone would complain, "We never see you anymore. When're you coming over?" His voice strident with injury.

Baffled by the unreality of their relationship, Daria choked on her words. She pictured her father seated in the old kitchen by the telephone, all his assumptions intact. Hearing his heavy breath through the wires she felt his menace. Yet, she could still not wholly connect him with the predator of her memories.

Sometimes, she imagined denouncing him to his face, watching his expression turn to astonishment. Then alarm. But she foresaw, too, his coarse features breaking quickly into artful innocence, his blue eyes bright with incredulity. Impossible to break through his practiced, impenetrable guile, she told herself and began to sink under the burden of knowledge.

∽⊶

Yet, her despondency was tempered by happiness, by delight with her surroundings: the manicured lawns, the resplendent trees, the grand houses, the quiet suburban streets. This is where I live, she whispered to herself, startled each day anew by the wonder of Jake, of Hannah, of home. Her present life shone so brightly, in fact, that its brilliance seemed at times to obliterate the past, leaving her in the end with a kind of vacancy, her mind unable to reconcile her disparate realities.

Gradually, however, she found herself bombarded by images, not of her childhood, not of her adolescence, but of her young adulthood. And as she recalled the misery of those desperate years, the years before Jake, when she was a twice divorced, self supporting single mother, she began to feel restless, agitated. Even into her thirties, she thought bitterly, she'd been the perennial innocent, a pushover for men like Dr. Berg, her unscrupulous analyst turned lover. With what cunning this man, fifteen years her senior, in whom she'd placed all her trust, had seduced her. With what shrewd manipulations kept her in thrall for years. How malleable she'd been! How gullible! And why had she been such easy prey, she asked herself. Wasn't it because she'd been seasoned for victimhood? Rendered blind to danger by the malefactions of her own duplicitous father? Thrown into the world impaired, without armor, unequipped to discern evil?

All at once, she saw the anguish of her twenties -- the suicide attempts, the hospitalization, the dangerous men, all streaming together like rivulets converging into a single stream, a stream that flowed directly toward her father. She felt, then, a mental click, as if her divided brain had snapped suddenly together and two distinct images converged into one. In a flash, she saw him -- unmasked. Indivisible. Her father! Her assailant! One and the same man!

Trembling, she rushed to her desk and began to write in a kind of fever, the words erupting from her pen. She accused her father of years of sexual abuse, denouncing him as a criminal. "And you, my mother," she wrote, "did nothing to protect me." She blamed them for having thrown her into the world defenseless, an easy target for wolves. She closed with a warning -- if her father ever came near her again she'd call the police.

She sealed the letter, ran to the corner mailbox and released it from her hand as if it were a hot ember. Back home, she looked wildly around. The walls, the furniture, the floors, everything seemed glaringly bright, as if a film had dropped from her eyes. She felt shaky, but the house sustained her, belying as it did her alternate reality.

※

How odd, she thought days later, that she'd sent the damning letter without considering the consequences, as if her brain had shut down the moment the envelope had left her hands. What had she expected from her parents, she wondered in the aftermath of her mother's retaliatory response? That they'd weep in repentance? Rally to her support?

When she'd spotted an envelope addressed in Bronya's handwriting at her door Daria's hopes swelled. Her mother had never written to her before, and she read the single page greedily, unable to immediately decipher Bronya's European scrawl and broken English. But the moment she did make out her mother's message, an image of her -- small and stocky-- hurling a spear in her direction, popped into her mind.

Bronya accused her of telling "ugly, vicious, malicious lies," which, she said, nearly gave them both heart attacks. She'd lived through Hitler, the war, Siberia, but nothing, she wrote, not even the murder of her parents, was as terrible as what she was doing to them now. "Your father is a good, hard working man," she claimed, adding that they'd both always tried to give her everything, which "you never appreciated." She closed with, "Don't call us and we won't call you. Pretend we moved away."

※

With her mother's letter a fresh wound in her mind, Daria's first thoughts were for Hannah. But she was struck, too, by her own persistent naiveté, her almost eerie inability to anticipate the obvious. How was it possible that she'd not foreseen her mother's denials? Her hostility? It was as if her mind was still repudiating painful truths. Truths made the more onerous by the contradictory demands posed by her parents' embattled history. In contrast to their suffering her own troubles had always seemed inconsequential. And pity had invariably trumped suspicion. Loathing given way to empathy. So that even now, when she'd faced the worst about her father, her denunciations made her seem monstrous in her own eyes.

Nevertheless, she could not help but gloat over the vision of his near apoplexy at the sight of her lethal words, his shock at having been found out at last. For years, she thought, he must've lived in terror of exposure. She recalled his bowed head in the hospital visiting room after her breakdown, and his drunk driving accident after the collapse of her second marriage, when he'd killed a man and barely escaped imprisonment.

And yet, miraculously, year after year, he'd gone undetected -- with never a hint of suspicion. How he used to scrutinize her face, she remembered, trying to fathom her state of mind, to weigh his own peril. But not once had he seen blame in her eyes, detected distrust in her demeanor. So that, finally, he'd allowed himself to believe that she knew nothing, was, on that score, entirely without memory. Daria imagined his relief at the discovery, his gratitude. And, after years of repentance his certainty that he'd been absolved. Was out of danger.

To be found out now, at his advanced age, after a life time of silence, with his iniquities far behind him, must've stunned him. Her letter in hand, he'd probably trembled, gaped in horror -- felt as if an avenging angel had, indeed, descended upon him at last.

Daria rejoiced at the picture.

ॐ

The arrival of a second letter from Mimi took her by surprise. "Do you want to kill mom and dad?" it began. "I don't know what you think you're doing, but couldn't you be a little more kind, a little less cruel?" For two pages Mimi pleaded for mercy for the parents who, she claimed, may have wronged her but had nevertheless tried their best.

To this Daria replied that she understood only too well the need for delusion, having been so long deluded herself.

Then, nothing more.

CHAPTER FOUR

As months passed with no word from her family the world appeared to Daria increasingly stark. Desolate. As if the sky had been stripped of some essential radiance. Gradually, as she began to grasp the depth of her own isolation, she started to question the wisdom of her life long pursuit of truth, to wonder if her insistence on reality hadn't been a mistake. All along she'd been driven by the belief that the world's empathy would flow from enlightenment. But the longer her relatives' silence about Ivan persisted, the more she felt betrayed by the very principles to which she'd so zealously adhered. She'd foreseen something else, she realized. Something more. It was as if the program she'd pursued had been a course of study, at the end of which she'd expected a diploma. But now she understood that no awards would be forthcoming.

Often, in fact, the present seemed to her even more grievous than the past. As long as she'd kept her secret she'd never doubted that if all were known outpourings of sympathy would follow. But even at home her disclosure had elicited little more than a limp hug from Jake and hardly a shrug from Hannah, to whom she'd confided a sanitized version of the story.

With surprising rapidity the family fell into a new pattern. Hannah occasionally called her grandparents and Jake chauffeured her for infrequent visits. Daria had no contact with either them or Mimi. And for many months her daily life was marked by a sense of the surreal. In a single stroke she'd become a pariah both to her family and the world. At school, when talk among her colleagues, many of whom she'd known for years, turned to relatives, she became silent. Withdrawn. Feeling all the while her co-workers suspicions of her. Their censure.

She could confide only in Amelia, with whom, in their single days, she used to smoke pot while the children slept, their long talks often breaking into wild laughter or abandoned weeping. Both re-married now, they met weekly in a Manhattan restaurant, where Daria handed her the mock "Father's Day" poem she'd written: "Remember how you f_ _ _ _ _ me dad?"

Amelia read it and burst into tears. Nor was she wholly surprised. "You told me about it a long time ago," she said.

"I did? When was that?"

"Well, not exactly. But you kept alluding to it. Anyway, I knew there was something not kosher between you and your father."

"Incredible. I don't remember a thing."

"Of course not. We were both stoned out of our minds," Amelia said, at which they laughed raucously.

But after that day, whenever Daria again alluded to the subject, Amelia frowned and looked away.

Might illusion be, in fact, preferable to reality, Daria began to wonder. By pursuing truth hadn't she, like Oedipus, figuratively gouged out her own eyes? Been ostracized by her mother, her father, her sister? Deprived Hannah of her family?

∽∾

In time, however, Daria began to applaud herself, to realize that she'd risen above her upbringing.

Bronya had always looked down on Ivan as a coarse "Ruskie." The Polish Jews, she'd say, were more refined than the Russian Jews, and if not for the war she wouldn't have married a "savage" like Ivan. Trapped in Siberia, however, she'd had no choice but to hook up with a native Russian, someone who knew the system, could unearth food even in the worst of times, bring home chocolate while others starved. After the war, however, Bronya's Polish friends had urged her to leave the "Ruskie." But with a child to provide for, what could she do, she'd often lament.

Married to a man brought up under a godless regime, Bronya had had to carry the torch of Judaism alone. While Ivan mocked religion, she spoke to the children of Jewish values, history and culture. It was she who sent the girls to "Yiddishe shule," she who sang Yiddish songs, told Yiddish fables and extolled the great Jewish thinkers.

There was also an underside to Bronya's character, however. While she took great pains with her appearance, she was slovenly at home. And she was often vulgar, her store of Yiddish profanities equal to her stock of Yiddish witticisms. So frequently, in fact, had Bronya's expletives rained down on Daria she sometimes suspected her mother suffered from Tueret syndrome. She felt certain, in any case, that Bronya's slovenliness, her crude mouth, her vile relationship with her own sister all pointed to a broader familial and cultural decline.

As sole survivors of their large, extended family, one would've expected Bronya and her sister Chana to be devoted friends. But they hated one another. For years Bronya had lamented her sister's absence, urging her in every letter to immigrate to America from France, where she'd landed with her husband and two children after a failed attempt to reach Israel. Daria, too, had yearned for the aunt and cousins she no longer remembered, her imagination drawing rosy pictures of family life. Then, six years after the Khasmanovs' own emigration, the longed for event occurred -- Aunt Chana and her family were coming to New York!

Even before the family's arrival, however, Daria overheard tense, whispered conversations between her mother and father. "They'll expect miracles from me. They think everyone in America is rich," Ivan grumbled while Bronya wept.

From the beginning, relations between the families were strained and before long, outbreaks of animosity between the two sisters became routine.

What could explain this enmity between siblings who'd lost everything -- parents, brothers, relatives, home and country? Sisters who by every measure should've cherished and clung to one another? Did their mutual malice stem from the war or was it rooted in a more distant past, Daria wondered.

Bronya had fled Poland at nineteen, never again to see her parents or brothers, whose loss she still mourned -- particularly that of her beloved "mamishee."

"When you lose a mother you lose everything," she used to say.

But for Daria, this unknown grandmother had never been more than an abstraction. Nor could she understand how the devoted woman of Bronya's tales could've produced two such spiteful daughters as her mother and aunt. And while Daria shared her mother's grief over her murdered family, she'd long ago begun to form her own picture of them.

Not until adulthood did Daria learn of her maternal grandmother's Hassidic roots, the Hassidim being a fundamentalist sect peculiar for their insularity and outmoded attire. The men wore side curls and black suits, the married women long dresses and wigs. Breaking away from this extremist group must've been anguishing enough for the "mamishee," Daria thought. To then have both parents die prematurely and lose one sister to America and another to a distant town, must, indeed, have left her bereft.

Like her daughter after her, the mamishee, too, had quarreled with her only remaining sibling, who, as a pious Jew had refused to eat in her sister's house and had rarely visited. Nor had this religious sister liked her only son's preference for his aunt's secular home over his own.

These lost relatives had always been sharply etched in Daria's imagination but only as an adult did she begin to see parallels between them and their offspring. Like her mother, Bronya had lost both parents early on and like her, was left with only one sister with whom she was locked in discord -- the seeds of which, Daria now suspected, had been planted by the previous generation.

Even as a youngster Daria had questioned Bronya's adoring descriptions of her own mother. And in her grandparents' one surviving photograph she thought she found grounds for her skepticism. Formally dressed and stiffly posed in contemporary fashion, the couple appears attractive, prosperous. And in her grandmother's angular face Daria could see the likeness to Bronya. But most striking, she'd always thought, was the similarly severe demeanor in both the mother and daughter.

Certainly, this grandmother, parentless and at odds with both community and family had had ample cause for bitterness. Adding to her troubles, her charming, handsome husband had been a gambler whom she'd often had to hunt down and drag home. And pictorial appearances to the contrary, Bronya grudgingly admitted that the family had been so poor as to sometimes suffer from hunger.

In the face of loneliness, an unreliable husband, four children to bring up in impoverished circumstances, this grandmother, Daria surmised, far from being the nurturing woman Bronya liked to remember, probably had the sour disposition which gave rise to the life long enmity between her daughters.

Nor were the family parallels limited to the maternal side. Even as a youngster, Daria was struck by the resemblances between her mother's father and her own. Both were blond and fair complexioned, reputedly charismatic, good looking, and prone to card playing. While Daria never knew Ivan to indulge in this pastime, Bronya often related bitter tales of his gambling habits in the past -- the problem becoming so severe she'd threatened to leave him.

In light of this pattern of recurrence, Daria questioned whether her own suffering might not also have sprung from some more ancient source. Bronya had often claimed to have been her father's favorite, and while this was thin grounds on which to make a supposition, she knew generational repetition within incest families to be an established fact.

Not surprisingly, most perpetrators were also found to have a history of abuse. At age ten, after the untimely death of his own father, Ivan had been placed in an impoverished Soviet orphanage, where, Daria surmised, he might very likely have been molested.

She began to wonder, too, if the afflictions in her own family history might not reflect more large scale disorders. Persecution, anti-Semitism, poverty, these conditions had certainly poisoned the lives of East European Jews, and their survival, she thought, probably demanded a good measure of cunning and ruthlessness -- qualities she noted in all the refugees of her parents' circle. These people seemed never to trust or help one another and their relationships were often marred by envy and acrimony.

Growing up, Daria had marveled at the refugees' duplicity, how they might curse one another in private and embrace in public, or live hard scrabble lives behind closed doors but appear prosperous and jovial in full view. No one was more adept at this sham than Ivan, whose merriment at the immigrants' increasingly lavish celebrations was particularly excessive. Flushed and beaming, his eyes intoxicated, he'd pull Daria to him, and with shouts and laughter drag her around the floor. Bronya, in the meantime, would be off in a corner with one or more of her landsmen, her usually dour face all smiles and amiability. Or she'd be on the dance floor, waltzing in the arms of some man, a blissful expression on her artfully made up face.

Daria used to deplore these showy affairs. But in later years she could sympathize with the hunger of these uprooted people for at least the appearance of success. The memory of their constant milling about in the confined spaces of the displaced persons' camps in Germany, their incessant, agitated buzz, their frequent, loud quarrels -- these were seared into her child's mind. As an adult, therefore, she could understand her aunt's owning expensive furniture despite a near empty refrigerator. Or her mother's buying party finery while wearing one shabby skirt at home. She empathized, too, with her lost grandparents' pride in their costly furnishings even as they lacked food.

In pre-war Poland the Jews had lived hard, circumscribed lives. Their family and communal relations had been rife with concealment, innuendoes, feuds and intrigues. And after the war their offspring had brought this ghetto culture to America. Every family had its secrets and its skeletons. One youngster's father, it was whispered, was not his biological parent. Another refugee, it was said, had been a "Kapo" (guard) in the concentration camp.

And at the Khasmanov's, only the family knew that Ivan had been imprisoned for deserting the Russian army.

Prizing appearances as they did, these survivors also deluded themselves, so that for them fantasy and reality were often blurred. Bronya, for instance, always claimed her parents had been middle class but sometimes blurted that an orange had been a luxury. Or, she scorned Ivan on the one hand yet insisted he'd been a good husband and father on the other. It was this self willed blindness on her mother's part which had enabled Ivan to operate for so long with impunity, Daria had concluded, a failing for which she now held Bronya accountable

And hadn't, she, herself, also been brainwashed, Daria thought. Taught to disavow experience and embrace delusion? By finally rejecting pretence, then, hadn't she risen above her environment, escaped its depravities, its avarice and malice? In reasoning thus Daria found consolation for her loneliness.

As months of estrangement from her family turned into years she was surprised by her own increasing detachment. And after awhile, she began to notice that in passing the highway exit to her parents' home to and from work each day she felt little more than a lingering regret -- as if some inner nerve center had died. She felt morally removed, obligated to live by her own rules. Imprisoned by her isolation, she nonetheless pitied her mother's and sister's enslavement to delusion.

CHAPTER FIVE

A t the news of her father's fatal illness, Daria's first impulse was to flee. It'd been almost three years since she'd seen him – and his image had begun to fade, so that in her sturdy house, with husband and daughter, he'd become a ghost in the attic – disquieting but not debilitating. The sight of Hanna's stricken face, though, and her hoarse voice speaking the appalling words – lung cancer, brought him instantly back to life – his presence so palpable Daria wanted to run. In bed later she tried to summon thought. But none came. Bombarded by emotion, her brain seemed to shut down.

She awoke the next morning to shocked realization. And as her feet touched the cold floor she was gripped by the old dread. As if her father were still skulking about, stalking her.

Compelled to act, she felt unhinged, adrift in unnavigable waters. The women's group pulled her in, suggesting she meet with her parents accompanied by Jill, the social worker. Buoyed by the prospect of facing her mother and father in the company of an ally, Daria sent them a note.

Her mother's reply days later, offering to meet alone with her at Dr. Pearle's, came as a shock. Might Bronya actually be willing to hear her story, she wondered. This seemed hard to believe. Yet, she could see no other reason for her suggesting a meeting. And for days she looked forward to unburdening herself at long last to the mother from whom she'd never before received solicitude.

When Dr. Pearle asked her what she expected from this meeting, however, she could only mumble incoherently.

On the appointed day Daria sat in Dr. Pearle's office in a state of petrified alertness. At the first sight of her mother she felt a jolt. Given her father's illness and their own estrangement she'd expected Bronya to look distressed. Even haggard. Instead, she seemed surprisingly radiant -- so stylishly dressed and artfully made up that their separation, Daria thought with fleeting bitterness, seemed to have agreed with her. Stunned, Daria greeted her parent with only a nod, and facing her from the opposite end of the room with Dr. Pearle between them, she asked abruptly, "So you're ready to acknowledge that my father sexually abused me?"

A momentary silence. Daria stared defiantly ahead while Bronya looked down at her hands. She spoke, finally, tremulously, her tone impassive, as if she meant only to clarify some misconception, to shed new light on a minor disagreement. Mesmerized by her mother's bright appearance, Daria could not immediately focus on her words or grasp their meaning. They seemed to her random, unrelated to the matter at hand and she could only listen in bewilderment, catching no more than an occasional name or reference.

As Bronya went on speaking her voice became more fervent, more confident. She brought up Daria's childhood friend, Peggy, and her cousin Felicia. But to what end, Daria could not discern. She also referred repeatedly to Daria's long forgotten diaries, left in her old bedroom. And at the thought of her mother's small figure bent in some corner over her girlish scrawls Daria felt an odd stab of pity. Of remorse.

Finally, she began to perceive a pattern in her mother's discourse. To realize she'd come here, not to listen but to persuade. To tell her that the abuse she claimed to have suffered had never occurred. Because if "such a thing" had ever happened, wouldn't she, Daria, have told her friend, her cousin, her diary? Wouldn't some suggestion of it have appeared somewhere? But she'd searched everywhere, spoken to everyone and found, "Nothing. Absolutely nothing!" she declared.

Daria jumped up suddenly. "This meeting is over," she announced.

Bronya sat transfixed, speechless, and after a pause she noisily gathered her things. "You could at least say good bye," she groused as she headed toward the door.

Obdurate, Daria said nothing, but with her mother gone, she broke into raucous, uncontrollable laugher, water running from her eyes.

Back outdoors, she wandered blindly about and found herself lost, roaming unknown streets with an all too familiar feeling of panic.

In the days ahead Bronya's image intruded itself on her thoughts. She imagined her preparing for their meeting. Selecting her outfit. Having her hair done. Applying her make up. She pictured her mother's fraught journey into an unfamiliar part of the city, her search for the address among the rows of high risers, her trembling entrance into a strange environment, her anticipatory anxiety. And despite herself, Daria could not help but feel a measure of pride. Her mother had shown up, had looked attractive, had appeared poised. Nevertheless, Daria was prepared to renounce her. To let her image fade along with that of her father, whose fate no longer concerned her.

⚬⚭⚬

Daria had so far banished Ivan from memory, in fact, that hearing about him months later she was startled -- not by the news of his impending death but by the fact of his continued existence. So the day a sobbing Hannah delivered the fatal words, "Grandpa's dying," she was pained, not for her father, but for her daughter, whose grief she could not explain. From where had Hannah's woe sprung, Daria wondered – from a love for her grandfather? Unlikely, she thought. In all of Hannah's seventeen years Ivan had done little more than address her with the same few mocking phrases. So at the sight of her daughter's swollen eyes and tear stained face Daria berated herself for having wrecked the family.

She lay awake that night appalled by the consequences of her truth telling. Her mind bruised by the sight of Hannah's pain, she agonized anew over the wisdom of her confessions. Could one survive without the solace of fantasy, she wondered.

But it was too late for regrets. The spoken could not be unspoken. Now she debated whether to visit her dying father or not. If she did not, would she forever reproach herself? Wished she'd paid witness to his passing? But if she did see him, how was she to behave? He was beyond the reach of condemnation. Of accountability. Of confrontation. To rush to his death bed with her reproaches was unthinkable. What then? Could she enter his sick room with the appropriate expression of sorrow? Play the dutiful daughter? Impossible, she thought.

The next day her mind was flooded with thoughts of her

father. She visualized him in his hospital bed, frightened and in pain. She imagined his emaciated body, his gaunt face, his agonized moans, and she decided she must see him. She pictured herself driving to lower Manhattan. Negotiating traffic. Parking the car. Searching the long, sterile hospital halls for his room. She saw her mother, her sister, her brother-in-law, her aunt and uncle gathered in her father's room, visualized their dark, disapproving gazes as she approached his bed. She envisioned his prone, skeletal body under a thin blanket, saw his wasted face and sunken eyes turned to her. She imagined his wan smile, his frail hand reaching out, waiting for her pity. Her contrition. And she recoiled from the vision.

Still, she felt she must go. But not tomorrow. Or the next day. She was too busy, too exhausted. She'd go Friday -- if he were still alive. If not -- then the Fates would've decided.

When the phone rang late the next night she was surprised only by the voice at the other end. It was her uncle, a man who rarely spoke and had never learned English. "Your father died," he said in Yiddish.

"What time?" she asked incongruously. And when he told her, she said, "Thank you for letting me know," with a scrupulous politeness.

Jake lifted his head. "Who was that?" he said.

"My father's dead," she answered.

"Oh," he said, and turned back to sleep.

She lay awake, conscious of her reclined body and the deep warmth of the bed. Shouldn't there be something more, she thought. Shouldn't she talk? Weep? Wake Jake and demand he listen? But what was there to say? Her father had died and she felt nothing -- only a profound gratitude for the snug room and the comfort of Jake's body next to hers.

She woke the next morning to a strange sense of release, as if a storm had passed. But she was jealous of Hannah's grief. Startled by her own blankness, she searched herself for emotion, but found only questions. How had Ivan looked at the end? What had been his final words? Had he never asked for her?

When the funeral announcement arrived in the mail Daria felt only surprise. Having renounced her family she presumed they'd disowned her as well. But all week the funeral occupied her mind. She pictured the rabbi telling the mourners Ivan had been a good man. A hard worker. A devoted husband. A loving father. She visualized the group gathered at the cemetery, watching the coffin being lowered into the ground. She imagined first her mother, then her sister throwing the customary shovel of dirt into the grave. She saw her father, dressed in his one suit, lying face up in the closed coffin, his cold body about to be laid in the ground.

She imagined people arriving at her mother's house later to "sit shivah," (mourn) and she wondered what she would tell them about her missing elder daughter.

My father's dead, she told herself daily yet she felt everywhere his coarse presence. As palpable as if he were still alive. Could she not grasp his death because she'd not witnessed his dying, she asked herself. And was she doomed, then, to live in limbo -- unable to either mourn him or absorb his demise?

As her daily life went on without interruption Daria understood the importance of ceremony, of convention. For her, Ivan's death had been met with silence. Routine. There'd been no phone calls, no rites, no tears, no gatherings -- no activities to mark the occasion. For weeks she felt guilty, obligated to inform at least one person of her father's passing. But she could find nothing to say about him that would not elicit aversion. Condemnation.

With Ivan gone, though, she looked forward to reconciling with her mother and sister. Now that his tyranny was at end, Daria thought, surely her relatives would summon her, make amends for their coldness, their ill treatment. And she dreamed of their becoming once more a family.

Weeks passed with no word from her mother or sister. At first, Daria felt only bewildered. But as days of silence became months, her bafflement turned into dread. Was it possible Bronya and Mimi had repudiated her for life, that they would never be willing to acknowledge Ivan's guilt? The idea startled her into a cold alertness.

When a year of estrangement became two, Daria's sense of void had become so habitual as to seem almost normal. And while she dreamed of reunion, she also reveled in her new found firmness, her own clarity in the face of her family's ongoing state of delusion.

Yet, with the passing of another year, the lengthiness of the divide began to rankle and alarm her. The despot, after all, was long dead. And while she understood her relative's abhorrence of truth, she'd not anticipated the ease with which they might give her up. Her resolve, though, she thought, was equal to theirs. Unless they acknowledged her injuries she'd let them go. This was the message she'd instructed Hannah to deliver to her grandmother.

On the day Hannah announced, "Grandma is ready to talk," Daria ran to the phone. She hadn't spoken to her mother in six years and she expected an emotional exchange. But the conversation that followed was surprisingly curt, resulting only in their agreeing to meet the following day at Bronya's house.

The next afternoon Daria drove toward her old home in a state of frenzy, expecting to walk into a cauldron of emotion. She first spotted her mother standing with folded arms at the open front door, and she bounded up the steps, her tears in readiness. But Bronya remained grimly silent, her face expressionless.

After an abrupt "hello," Daria strode past her into the living room, sat down in a corner chair and turned expectantly toward her. Bronya, however, said nothing, and for awhile the two women only regarded one another coldly. Incongruously, Daria found herself assessing Bronya's appearance: her hair, her make-up, her clothing, and, thinking, oddly, that her mother had dressed for the occasion. A kind of torpor seemed, then, to come over her and for a moment, she wondered if she could summon the energy to deal with her parent at all.

Rousing herself, she shed what instantly felt like fabricated tears which, nevertheless, broke the silence. "Why are you crying?" Bronya, seated on the edge of the sofa, asked coolly. Daria shut up abruptly, a chill running through her veins. Stymied by her parent's detachment, she sat up straight and launched into her prepared speech, all the while conscious of her mother's icy scrutiny.

Her father, Daria said, had begun molesting her at a very young age, raping her repeatedly throughout her childhood and adolescence. And all their years of family misery and upheavals, she wound up heatedly, were outcomes of this ongoing, secret abuse.

To these claims Bronya listened without expression, in uncharacteristic silence, neither raising objections nor desiring elaboration, as if her attentiveness were merely a pose. And as she went on speaking Daria, too, began to feel distracted, to stare at the front door and imagine herself running from the house.

It was not until she brought up her own accusatory letter that her mother became suddenly animated. These allegations against Ivan, Bronya said with a flash of heat, had hit them like a sledgehammer, practically knocking them off their feet. "Whoever heard of such things? Who in their wildest dreams would think of such a thing?" she said in a shocked tone. "When I questioned him he turned into a wild animal, threatened to run away to Florida. Do you know what this means?" she demanded in Yiddish. "He was going to take half the money. Half the money! What would be left, then, do you think? What would I live on? We didn't have so much that I could live on half. Did you want I should live in the street?" she shouted, her mouth twisted in venom.

Speechless, Daria shrank back, picturing her mother a ragged bag lady sleeping on a park bench. But finding her voice again, she retaliated: "You didn't protect me. You didn't care about me." She began to shriek, to feel feverish, to sob.

But Bronya only reiterated that she'd known nothing. "If I knew such a thing! If I knew he was doing such a thing to my child I would've killed him. I would've had him deported. I would've thrown him in jail. But such a thing! Who could think of such doings? Who could've imagined this! He seemed so innocent. So ignorant. Whoever even talked about sex? We were ashamed. Embarrassed. Such things no one talked about. I knew nothing. Absolutely nothing," she insisted, her eyes flashing.

She claimed, nonetheless, to have urged Ivan to contact his daughter, to speak to her about the accusations. "If someone had said such things about me I'd want to know why," she'd told him.

"So what did he say?" Daria asked, picturing Ivan's alarm, his evasions.

"Such things you can't force," he'd responded, and when pressed, claimed he'd, "never touched the child," threatening to run off if he weren't believed.

Daria left her old home that afternoon feeling oddly disjointed, unable to connect herself to the person who'd for so long lived in it. And while she felt vaguely gratified -- her mother *had* voiced anger, shock, horror -- and before his death, she *had* urged Ivan to speak to his daughter -- she couldn't help but wonder if this meager exchange between them was all there was to be. She was puzzled, too, by Bronya's defending herself against a charge she'd never made, shuddering at the implications of her mother's protesting too much that she'd known "absolutely nothing."

At the same time, her mother's fears of being thrown out into the streets stung her to the quick. And driving away that day she wondered at her own failure to consider Bronya's limited resources, a failure which seen in the light of her own prosperity made her now appear callous, self-centered. She resolved, then, to make amends, to take care of her mother, convinced that such restitution would heal them.

Thus, she once more took up her old role as her mother's companion, her confidant, her drudge. And everywhere they went, in the streets, in stores and restaurants, people smiled at them, signaled their approval. "These years we didn't talk, it was like I lost my right eye. Now I feel like I have it back," Bronya blurted one day. And Daria, feeling a rush of gratitude, turned to her expectantly. But there was nothing more.

"I always knew 'the mamishee' would take care of me. And now, here you are," Bronya declared on another occasion, her eyes turned heavenward. At which Daria could only stare in astonishment.

                                      ∽◇∾

Reconciled with her mother, Daria expected at long last to find a friend in her sister. But her conciliatory letter to Mimi was met with censure. "I was there when dad was dying, where were you? I was there when mom suffered anxiety attacks, where were you?" Mimi wrote. In letter after letter she upbraided Daria for a host of derelictions. She'd deprived her sons of family, carried off their niece, abandoned her mother and father, reneged on her family responsibilities.

Daria read these reproaches in amazement, stunned by Mimi's disregard for Ivan's crimes. "I resent your trying to get me to validate your view of things. That may have been your experience, but it wasn't mine!" she wrote in one of her letters. And in another, "I'm sorry, if as you claim, your life was such hell but I actually have some fond memories of the past which nothing you can say will change, so stop trying to turn me into you!"

Bronya, in the meantime, managed to avoid any imputation of responsibility for the rupture between her girls, appearing even to delight in her own intermediary role. "Look at this," she might say, in an amused tone. "My daughters are so alike and yet they're not talking to one another."

There were even moments when Daria had the distinct impression that far from promoting a reconciliation between herself and Mimi, Bronya sought to prolong their hostilities. "The boys don't have to know anything," she whispered darkly on several occasions, as if she were warding off some evil spirit. Daria, hearing her own self loathing echoing in her ear, was stunned into silence.

∽∾

And just as Bronya managed to conceal her own role in the ongoing family friction, she was able to dodge all of Daria's attempts to bring up the past. "Do you want to kill me," she'd gasp, clutching her chest. Or, she'd remark in Yiddish, "The whole of life is worth nothing," thus squelching Daria's troublesome allusions.

CHAPTER SIX

The sisters met for the first time at a family wedding. When the ornate invitation arrived in the mail Daria felt a mild shock; she hadn't heard from these relatives in years. But this affair, she realized, was an opportunity for her and Mimi to meet at last. Standing face to face, she thought, they were bound to embrace, to let all grievances melt away.

Hannah, too, was delighted with the invitation, and the three of them headed toward the event on that brilliant June afternoon feeling like outcasts reinstated into society.

Inside, Daria searched for a familiar face among the crowd, expecting at every moment to run into her sister. When she and Mimi did almost collide outside the ladies' room, Daria instantly threw herself on her with a squeal. But Mimi only mumbled inaudibly and walked away, remaining surprisingly invisible for the remainder of the afternoon.

She needs time, Daria thought vaguely, amazed by her sister's aloofness, her coldness even at close proximity.

When Bronya began spending summer week ends with her and Jake in their Catskill home, a short drive from Mimi's own cabin, Daria confidently awaited what she thought would be the inevitable reunion. Yet, week after week there was still no word from Mimi, so that it seemed, Daria thought with growing disbelief, that her sister *did* want a permanent estrangement.

Bronya, however, continually chatted about Mimi, her husband, her sons, as if there'd been no falling out between the families.

"What the hell's going on?" Daria demanded finally of her mother, venting her rage with such vehemence, Jake came running in alarm.

The following week a note arrived from Mimi expressing a willingness to meet.

∽◌◌

Days later, Daria sat alone in her mother's house taking in the peeling paint, the stained carpet, the worn sofa. How shabby everything looks, how neglected, she thought with remorse. Yet, at the sight of the familiar disarray, her mother's make up on the dining room table, the damp towels hanging from the banister, she wanted also to flee.

She was here waiting for Mimi. Startled anew by her sister's uncanny resemblance to herself, apparent in the photograph on the table, she thought poor Mimi -- forced for so long to play the role of the eldest, she'd come, finally, to look like her.

When her sister opened the front door Daria ran to her with open arms but Mimi dodged her embrace. At the table, she sat coolly silent while Daria fawned over her. "Don't you see?" Daria kept shouting in the face of Mimi's mute scowl. "Can't you understand?" she pleaded

"I was O.K. with the way things were. We got along just fine without you," Mimi exploded finally.

In the face of which Daria's pleas became more heated, more desperate.

∽∾

They met twice more with little variation. Daria begged while Mimi fumed. "They said you were lying -- or crazy. Now what am I supposed to think?" she screamed.

Only when the talk turned to Ivan's illness did Mimi relent. "How had he looked? What had he talked about? Had he known he was dying?" Daria asked.

Mimi described their father's emaciated body, his constant pain, his pleas for morphine, his decreasing lucidity. They talked of him in a hushed way, as if he were still alive and they were standing beside his bed while he slept. As she listened, Daria pictured him -- his gaunt frame, his nude scalp, his hollow cheeks -- the images so sharp it was almost as if she and her sister stood together in the hospital room, sharing, finally, the emotions of siblings at the approach of their father's death. For a moment, their old bond seemed to reassert itself and Daria ventured to ask, "Did he mention me?"

At which Mimi lowered her gaze. "No," she mumbled. Shamefacedly, Daria thought. "He was in so much pain all he cared about was morphine. That was all he asked for," she added hurriedly, with a hint of remorse.

She's lying, Daria thought, but she sensed the fib was a protective one. Even on his death bed, she suspected, Ivan had vilified her, called her crazy -- which seemed cruelest of all, suggesting as it did a chilling depth of indifference. Had he never longed to confess, yearned for repentance, she wondered.

Once again her father began to haunt her mind, his disembodied head appearing before her eyes. He seemed to be beckoning her, looking either wide eyed, his face lit by a hectic glow, or pale and pitifully drawn.

"Why am I seeing him? He's dead and buried," she complained to Dr. Pearl, who, in her usual mild way only asked, where? The question startled her. She realized she didn't know where her father lay interred.

At home she frantically tracked down the funeral announcement and stared at it, undecided. The cemetery, she guessed, was far out on Long Island, perhaps several hours drive from home. But she understood all at once that she had to go there, had to see the ground in which her father lay and the stone that bore his name.

She imagined this trip as a kind of pilgrimage which she and Mimi would undertake together. She pictured them standing arm in arm at the grave, weeping and consoling one another. When she declared her intention to go, however, Mimi responded with a sharp, "Yes. *You* should go." To which Daria could only murmur her assent.

Everything about the trip alarmed her. The traveling alone. The distance. The unfamiliar roads. The being at the graveside on her own.

Her women's group urged her to go, to curse her father and spit on his grave.

She set out finally one fall day. The sky shone bright blue and multicolored leaves dotted the road sides. Gradually, as she drove further and further into rural Long Island and her anxiety began to subside, she found herself almost enjoying the excursion. After awhile, as the highway narrowed, turned wooded and became a quiet country road she thought only of mundane things, her

destination blotted from her mind. Cheered by the sunlight and
the bucolic scene, she began to feel even serene, pleased to be out
driving on such a day.

But when the road widened and she spotted tombstones
dotting the fields, her heart began to clamor. Searching for the
name "Beth Shalom," she passed one vast cemetery after another.
And as the rows of monuments went on mile after mile with no
"Beth Shalom" in sight she began to panic, to think about all the
thousands of corpses rotting in the ground and to wonder how,
with so many coffins piled up over the centuries there could still
be room for the living.

She turned, at last, into a parking lot surrounded by empty
fields then headed toward the site's only building, a grim cement
block structure. Stepping from bright daylight into a dim,
cavernous interior, she felt disoriented, fearful. After a moment
she made out open shelves, a low wide counter and a lone woman
seated with her back turned, behind it. She approached cautiously
and in a faltering voice began to say she was looking for uh…

"Name of deceased?" the woman asked brusquely, then removed
a long black ledger from an open shelf and began to leaf through
it. Daria watched, mesmerized by the designations appearing
beside each name in the columns, hardly able to grasp that these
markings had anything to do with her father. But there he was --
Ivan Khasmanov – A12, written into the book of the dead.

Lightheaded, confused by the woman's curt directions, she
made her way out the door. Clutching the cemetery map, she
walked aimlessly, imagining her father's spirit overhead. "Bist du?"
(You're here), she heard him say, his mocking, pitiful expression
both repellent and beseeching. The wind beat her face and whipped
her hair. She saw no one.

Squinting at the small, indecipherable signs at the end of

each lane she thought in alarm she might never find her way and wondered vaguely why she'd come alone. "Yes. I'm here," she shouted in silent fury, her body pushing against the wind. Relieved at the sight of a lone woman bent over a grave in the distance, she ran toward her, asked apologetically for help and with confused voices clamoring in her head found her way.

When she spotted her father's tombstone, his engraved name jumped out at her. She stared at it hungrily and in disbelief, the inscription, "Loving husband. Loving father," a bitter sight for her eyes. She walked on the grave and around it, visualizing her father's coarse face, his smirk, the intoxicated gleam in his eyes. What would he think if he could see her here, she wondered. That she'd forgotten? That she'd forgiven? She shuddered at the thought. She shouted curses. Spit. Kicked the dirt under which he lay. She brought up sobs. Shed tears. But to no avail. She felt nothing. It was as if some inner wires had been cut and she could feel no emotion for her father.

Finally, there was no more reason to stay yet she couldn't bring herself to leave. She sat down on the ground and stared at her father's inscribed name, thinking she'd failed. She'd expected to be flooded by feelings. But she was hollow. Wooden. All that remained now was to find some parting gesture.

Her father had defiled her. Had lacerated her heart and broken its springs. Yet, he was dead and she was alive. "I'm alive. I'm alive!" she called to the heavens and walked away.

∽⌒∾

In the weeks that followed, Daria found herself at a crossroad. Her two years' devotion to her mother had not led to increased intimacy. On the contrary, Bronya resisted talk of the past with such tenacity that Daria began to suspect her of mere pretense in acknowledging Ivan's guilt in the first place.

She wondered now if her faith in eventual family solidarity was as ill founded as her expectations of her mother -- whether the silence at the heart of their family life might be permanent – a possibility she couldn't bear to contemplate. Yet, she could no longer overlook Bronya's remorselessness, her indifference. Nor could she deny that she hated her mother.

Their relationship was little more than a charade. Still, it seemed less painful to go on as they were than to incur another break. Bronya, Daria reasoned, would probably not live much longer, and she still hoped her ministration would one day win over her sister. Curiously, however, rather than limiting her involvement with Bronya as time went on, Daria found herself driven to do more and more for her. So that after awhile, she was once again inexplicably locked into the kind of servitude to her parent she'd so much resented as a girl.

∽◌∽

After Bronya suffered a mild heart attack while vacationing in Florida, Daria, home on sabbatical, volunteered to fly down and accompany her home. When she arrived at Bronya's condo, she found her in bed, holding court. For two days visitors crammed into the studio apartment while Daria, always mystified by her mother's hold over people, looked on in fascination, gradually beginning to understand how her mother managed to draw people out, tap into their deepest feelings, win their confidence and with sly seduction, bind them to her.

Again, Daria found herself the unwilling recipient of praise for her mother, obliged to nod and smile in the same false way she'd always hated as a youngster. During the two days she and Bronya were closeted together in close quarters, Daria found her particularly repugnant. Bronya hadn't bathed in a week and admitted frankly that she stank. Helping her mother wash, Daria held her breath against the stench. At night she lay in restless agitation on a cot beside her, struggling with violent emotions.

Yet, she couldn't help but feel warmed by the approving smiles of Bronya's admiring friends and to question her own perverseness in failing to distinguish in her mother the woman so beloved by others.

On the trip home Bronya clung to her. She clutched her arm at the airport, gripped her hand on the plane and whimpered at every bit of turbulence, so that for the duration of the flight Daria had to coax and console her. On disembarking, when a woman whispered from behind, "If that'd been me, I'd have clobbered her one," she surprised herself by coming to her mother's defense.

Back in New York, months of medical appointments followed. Seated with Bronya in countless waiting rooms, buoyed by Mimi's imagined approval of her conduct as well as the empathetic glances of patients and staff, Daria could almost convince herself she loved her mother. Yet, she could not shake off feelings of fraudulence and dared not admit to herself that she anticipated Bronya's upcoming heart surgery, not as an ordeal, but as a chance for intimate conversation with Mimi.

On the scheduled day, Daria arrived at the hospital in a fever of anticipation. And the moment she and Mimi sat down together in the waiting room, she launched into her prepared speech. Encouraged by Mimi's silence, broken only by her repeated urgings to, "Keep your voice down," Daria's monologue became increasingly heated, increasingly reckless. She heard herself laughing, talking excitedly, while everything in the vast room

-- the scattered figures, the brown furniture, the white walls --
seemed to whirl by in a blur.

When she spotted the surgeon in his bloodied smock standing
at the edge of the room and heard him calling out her mother's
name, Daria looked around in confusion, wondering for a moment
where she was. Thrown abruptly back into the hospital setting
she could hardly believe that hours had passed and her mother's
surgery was over. Feeling mildly dizzy as she and Mimi stood
dutifully listening to the doctor, she had difficulty following his
words, and found herself thinking absurdly that he seemed to be
looking beyond them as he spoke, as if he were searching for a
larger audience to applaud his work.

The operation, he said, had gone well and their mother was
in intensive care, where they could see her, but only briefly. To
this Daria nodded, keeping up her somber expression. Dazed,
she followed Mimi to the elevator. They rode in silence, their eyes
lowered, like two strangers thrown together in forced intimacy.

When, after endless instructions, signings in, donning of
smocks, they entered the intensive care unit, Daria gasped. There
was her mother -- splayed out on a hospital stretcher like a small
whale, a jumble of crisscrossing wires attached to ominous looking
machines extending from every part of her body, so that with her
bluish complexion, she looked more mechanical than human.
"Shocks you, doesn't it," Mimi said with what seemed to be
a triumphant smirk. Daria felt her heat rise but said nothing.
She watched dumbly as Mimi stroked one of Bronya's discolored
fingers with an expression of such tenderness Daria wondered
whether she did, in fact, love their mother.

But during the ensuing ten days of Bronya's hospitalization,
Mimi appeared at her side only once then left hurriedly. Running
beside her in the parking lot, Daria remarked, "What a pain in

the ass she's being," trying to strike that mocking tone about their mother familiar to them both. But Mimi only quickened her pace. "Not only does she have me jumping through hoops for her, she's got me doing errands for her roommate," Daria desperately quipped. "Well. Bye," she called as Mimi, unresponsive, stepped into her car.

Daria trekked back to the hospital weighed down by misgivings. Being at her mother's bedside, she had to admit, gave her a sense of normalcy, even importance. She imagined the idyllic picture the two of them must present -- the daughter accompanying her mother on her slow, laborious walks through the hospital halls, escorting her to the bathroom, demonstrating breathing into the "heart balloon," running for this, fetching that. How the other patients must envy the two of them their closeness, she thought. What pictures of family accord the sight of them must evoke.

Bronya's roommate, Mary, as well as her daughter, Susan, always spoke to Bronya deferentially. Susan, who was constantly embracing her own mother and often stretched out beside her in bed, her great mass squeezing the elder woman to the wall, seemed even to envy Daria *her* mother -- sensing perhaps a superior intellect.

Seated hour after hour in the small, close room, Daria imagined blurting the truth about Bronya, imagined the women's shocked expressions if she were to disabuse them of their illusions.

Still, leaving her mother's side at the end of the day she had to admit to a certain contentment, as if she'd been seduced by her own performance. How much simpler it was to go along, to be carried by the strong current of appearances. How much less wearying than always taking up arms.

And who, after all, was to say that her faithfulness was not, in fact, the truer reality? How solid it all was, how substantial

-- being at her mother's side, holding her arm, helping her breathe, talking to nurses, attending to this and that. Wasn't this physicality the more real, she asked herself. Weren't her memories, her knowledge, her feelings mere abstractions, lacking in material presence? If she did, indeed, present a convincing portrait of filial loyalty, then might not her actions be more authentic than her feelings, she thought.

The day she and Jake brought Bronya home from the hospital, Daria's constancy seemed to be rewarded. Mimi and Steven greeted them at their mother's door. Neighbors arrived with steaming pots of food and soon the atmosphere turned almost festive. What with the constant ringing of the phone, people streaming in, the lively conversation, Daria could not help but be struck by the seeming harmony of the picture, the ordinariness. She imagined people's disbelief if they learned that this group had, in fact, not come together in over seven years.

Despite everything we *are* a family, she thought.

CHAPTER SEVEN

Swept up in a tide of normalcy Daria could say, "I'm running to my mother's," which she regularly did, having slipped back into her old role as the eldest.

Mimi gushed over the caregiver she and Jake had hired. "If she can get along with that beauty queen she deserves a medal," Mimi mocked. Was this an oblique declaration of gratitude, Daria wondered. Seeing cause for cheer, she began making plans to reunite Hannah, due home for spring break, with her aunt. "You deprived me of my niece," Mimi had recently charged. Struck by the injustice of this claim, Daria had nevertheless felt culpable, and she leapt at the chance to make amends.

She decided on a theater party for the three of them, and as she purchased tickets and made arrangements, she felt herself in the grips of a rising excitement. After a seven year separation Hannah leapt at the suggested reunion, seeing in it, Daria knew, a restoration of the family life they both craved.

Aware of the significance of the occasion, they drove to Mimi's house in Queens feeling charged up. Elated. And when aunt and niece met they instantly hit it off, embracing one another with a fervor Daria could only envy. At the bus stop, where they waited for the express into Manhattan, the reunited pair stood chatting like old school friends, as absorbed in one another as if there weren't twenty-two years between them. For awhile, Daria looked on with amusement, delighted to have brought the two together. But when the bus was late, she started to pace, to glance at her watch. And as Mimi and Hannah went on chattering unconcernedly, she began to feel vaguely excluded.

True, it was she who'd left their little group to walk up and down the block, but even when she stood beside them, she felt somehow out of place, like a sole adult accompanying a couple of youngsters, or, as if, she thought wryly, she were the mother and they two the siblings. As she continued pacing, checking her watch, and straining for a glimpse of the delayed bus, she sensed, even, that her sister and daughter were whispering about her, secretly mocking her.

Standing apart, she felt mildly humiliated, a feeling she tried to shrug off. But when the exclusive tête-à-tête between aunt and niece persisted throughout the trip, as well as during the meal, she wondered what, exactly, Mimi was up to. And when she paid the bill, finally, for the tasteless, over priced lunch, she momentarily regretted the excursion, little knowing that a precedent had now been set which she'd come deeply to regret.

∽∽

With her mother fully recovered, Daria began taking her on shopping trips. Bronya loved to shop, to run her fingers over fabrics and evaluate their softness. She hated anything coarse against her skin and always shivered a little at the prospect. She could reject garments at a glance. In Bloomingdale's, Daria ran around loading clothing on her arms, shouting, "Look at this," or, "How about this," while Bronya wandered among the racks, amazed.

At the check out counter they often fell into conversation with the saleswoman, who nodded and smiled at them. "This is my daughter. She's buying me all this," Bronya would say with a flourish. The clerk invariably spoke, then, of her own mother, and the three of them had a moment of intimacy, of well being.

At the Bloomingdale's cafeteria Bronya would seat herself heavily at the table. "Oy vay," she'd sigh, then eat her hot lunch with relish, remarking occasionally, "Why don't you eat? You're hardly eating," continuing, then, to chat about her new neighbor or the woman she'd met that morning on the bus. But Daria would swallow her resentment, recalling the early years, when her mother owned only one skirt.

"Remember this. Look how beautiful it looks. All my friends ask me, where do I buy such beautiful clothes? But, of course, they'd never spend this kind of money," Bronya would often say with a smug smile. So as time went on Daria found herself buying more and more for her mother.

She liked to think her generosity to Bronya would soften Mimi toward her. But Mimi seemed, instead, oddly baffled and annoyed. As if, Daria thought, her benevolence to their mother was somehow a rebuke to herself. But Daria continued to catch at the slightest hope. So, when she and Jake moved to Manhattan her mind glowed with visions of family get togethers in their elegant Park Ave. apartment.

For Hannah's home comings everyone arrived in a festive mood, with the three cousins particularly happy with their restored relations. But Daria always worked herself into frenzy. "Sit down already," everyone shouted as she ran around tending to things. Yet Daria only quickened her pace and laughed the harder. "Remember when we were kids, we'd...," she'd shout at Mimi, hoping to ignite a spark of intimacy. But Mimi only mumbled and looked away.

By the end of such a visit Daria would feel drained, disappointed, suspicious of all their loud merriment.

But the day Mimi blew up at her, Daria was startled by her vitriol. She'd called that morning to say stormy weather would prevent them from keeping a luncheon date. When Daria worried aloud about the spoiled meal, Mimi shouted, "Take the fucking food and bring it here," slamming down the receiver. Stunned, Daria began to wonder if her sister's hostility might never be overcome, if her youthful antagonism, her shouts of "I hate you," had not, in fact, hardened into a permanent enmity.

Nevertheless, she continued to bring the family together. They always gathered in the same neighborhood restaurant in Queens. How charming, how enviable their little family must look, she thought as they exchanged gifts, laughed and embraced. At these gatherings, too, however, she felt overheated, restless, unable to curb her feverish chatter.

And the more the silence around her father deepened the more Daria thought of him. She'd picture his lean, weathered face with the hollow above his left eye where a bone had been removed, giving him a battered, thuggish look. Or she'd recall his stringy frame stretched out on the sofa in his underwear. He'd sleep on his back while the TV blared, his bare feet with their yellowed and cracked toe nails pointed straight up like a corpse, their foul odor filling the room. Or she'd see him lying on his side, exposing the gash running down his left thigh where'd he'd been shot in the war – the deep, ragged wound making him look mutilated. Pitiful.

She felt his eyes petitioning her – as if he were reaching out from the grave. He'd been dead six years, years which had come and gone without notice, without comment, as if he'd been erased from memory. Only she alone remained in the prison of his aura -- the sense of him -- watching, threatening, always with her.

Daria's work place, too, became freighted with fear. In the drab early hours, the antiquated school building had the look of a fortified penitentiary. The sky over the congested, industrial area was always polluted, always grey. Each morning Daria rushed past the restless teenagers milling around the front entrance, relieved to reach the safety of the interior. By afternoon, however, as students continued to congregate unchallenged in the halls, the unruliness within became as alarming as the rowdiness without. But the end of the day, when staff had to scurry past the hordes gathered outside the building, was invariably the most daunting time of all.

While early retirement brought relief, the more Daria saw of her mother and sister, the more she felt herself sinking again into a familiar mire. She considered calling once again on Dr. Freid, but picturing his seedy neighborhood, she hesitated. She thought, too, of Dr. Pearle's emphatic, "No," at the mention of his name, as well as her survivor group's wariness of male therapists. But in the end, she turned to the one person who'd helped her so much in her youth.

He was just as she remembered him -- short, stocky, bald, caustic and irreverent. For awhile she found his sarcasm humorous. "I'm sick and tired of hearing some of the most successful women in society complain about sexual abuse," he declared at the outset. At which Daria smiled, thinking he meant only to startle her out of her doldrums.

Whenever she mentioned Ivan, though, the doctor cut her off, as if the subject were irrelevant. And he railed against the women's movement. "Seeing child abuse as the root of all evil is bullshit," he said. "I know successful people who've come from the slums and losers who came from privilege. It's all in the genes. As far as I'm concerned nature trumps nurture every time. That's your problem. You blame everything on the abuse," he said.

For over a year Daria tolerated the doctor's pugnacity, finding it at times stimulating, even alluring. But when he remarked that, "Studies have shown a grown man can bring a fourteen year old to orgasm," or argued that she'd played a role in the incest and that her abusive father had also done her some good, she began to look more closely at the doctor's surroundings -- to wonder why he still lived in a small, shabby apartment filled with dilapidated furniture.

"What you're doing is not working for me," she declared one day.

"I have no agenda whatsoever," he replied

When Daria suggested she might be better off seeking help from a woman, the doctor became irate, denouncing female therapists in general and Dr. Pearle in particular with such force she imagined tearing up the check which lay between them and running from his office. "I'm quitting," she announced, at which point the doctor's shouts became so vehement that on her way out Daria stiffened in fear.

The next day, she wrote the doctor a note. "Eighteen months ago I came to you in good faith. But as I look back now, all the outcomes seem to me negative," she began, closing with the hope that he would not in the future treat women survivors of child sexual abuse, because, she wrote, "Your own rage against the feminist movement, of which you perversely persisted in addressing me as a spokesperson, poses a serious threat to their well being." Relieved to have hit on this measured tone, she sent the letter with a new sense of resolve.

"I always thought he was a bit mad," her friend Amelia said. "And he never let me talk about my father either.Whenever I tried, he'd shut me up," she added.

∽∾

Daria sent a note to Dr. Pearle and waited for a referral, continuing in the meantime, to pursue her relatives with a kind of manic fervor -- always over Jake's objections. "How can I abandon my elderly, sick mother," she'd argue.

In a recurring dream she sat alone in a restaurant, frantically waving across the room to where Bronya and Mimi sat together, but deep in conversation, they always ignored her.

"How's everybody?" Hannah would ask, calling from the midwest, and they would chat about Mimi, "the boys" and "grandma" in a breezy, intimate tone, as if theirs was a family like any other.

∽∾

Months passed with no word from Dr. Pearle. Finally, a call came from her daughter. Her mother, she said, suffered from Alzheimer's, the disease so far advanced she could no longer recognize her own children.

"My God! When did this happen?" Daria blurted.

They'd begun to notice the symptoms about ten years ago, the caller said. And Daria wondered vaguely what this meant.

For days afterwards she imagined encountering Dr. Pearle in the halls of some nondescript hospital, finding not the vibrant, youthful woman she'd known but a vacant, unseeing stranger.

The realization that the onset of Dr. Pearle's illness coincided with the start of her own therapy took hold of her gradually. First, she recalled heretofore inexplicable incidents: The doctor sobbing whenever she herself wept. The doctor blurting one day that her husband was having an affair with another woman and was leaving her. The long stretches of uncanny silences during their sessions.

In dreams Daria saw herself drifting in an ever widening pool of water, receding further and further from view.

She was standing alone on the corner of 86th and Broadway, waiting for Amelia, when she spotted her former lover crossing the street, his eyeballs protruding at the sight of her. When he passed her by and was about to enter a store, Daria called out recklessly -- "Ben."

He turned to her, abstracting his gaze.

"You probably don't recognize me with this hat on," she said, pulling it off.

In an instant, he was standing beside her, and with his arm firmly on her waist, he pulled her toward him.

Startled, she stepped away.

"I tried calling you," he blurted.

"Where?" she burst out.

"At the old number," he mumbled, looking down.

"We haven't lived there in a hundred years," she exclaimed, and checked a desire to say more.

He shot questions at her: What was she doing here? Who was she waiting for? When was her friend arriving?

Perplexed, Daria fired answers in return, feeling the old

familiarity flowing between them. He began talking in a low, rapid whisper, his mouth almost at her ear. He'd had prostate cancer, he said and, instantly, all her defenses collapsed. She began feeding him questions -- as if they were still intimate and almost twenty years hadn't elapsed.

Sighting Amelia, Daria waved her toward them, introduced her old flame to the friend who knew him only too well. But with no more than a nod, Ben continued talking more rapidly, with greater urgency, as if he wanted to fasten her to him. And as she stood listening, curious about the missing years, ("Has it been that long?" he said), she wondered why she lingered, why, in fact, she'd stopped him at all.

Yet, she let him talk, expecting at every moment the inevitable, "And you?" Wishing, after all, to tell him. But he went on and on, asking her nothing. So that she patted him, finally, and said with a mocking smile, "It's been really weird to see you," thinking as she turned away that he'd never spoken her name.

"I don't think he even knew who I am," she exclaimed to Amelia as they walked uphill, her heart curiously pounding.

"Oh, he knew you, all right," Amelia said.

"Still attractive, don't you think, even at his age?" Daria tossed out, and would've said more, but Amelia only muttered and changed the subject.

Later, Daria puzzled over Ben's interrogation of her, as if, she realized with a start, he'd suspected her of stalking him. She almost laughed out loud at the notion, wishing she'd quipped, "Don't flatter yourself," or, "There's no fool like an old fool." Since her move to Manhattan she'd often pictured this encounter, wondered how she'd feel. And standing close to him, hearing once more his low, breathy voice, she'd been momentarily charmed.

She marveled at Ben's claiming to have called her, and the possessive way he'd pulled her toward him. "Still up to your old tricks?" she wished she'd said, remembering at the same time the way he used to wrap her in his arms, hold her like a child against his ample masculinity – an embrace to which she'd become addicted. But the familiar, shabby cloak he'd worn made him look seedy, run down, as if his true nature could no longer be concealed.

But why had she been pulled so easily into his orbit, she asked herself. She'd wanted only to look at him, to gauge her own reactions to his presence. For a moment, she'd even imagined flaunting her success at him, relishing the chance to say, my daughter the doctor, my husband the financier, my Park Ave. apt. Instead, she'd felt immediately submerged by him, become in an instant a mere receptor for his outpourings.

Why had she been so overwhelmed by the sight of him, she wondered. Cloaked in his therapist role, he'd, after all, been no less a predator than her father. He'd flirted with her right from the start of their joint sessions with her ex-husband, Marvin, who'd been either too deranged or intoxicated to notice.

When the doctor had first leaned in for a kiss, she'd recoiled, and for awhile, she'd stayed away. But when Marvin's behavior became more erratic, more disturbing, she'd returned, and gradually, she'd been drawn into an affair with Ben from which she'd struggled for years to extricate herself. Yet, now, some twenty years after their last meeting, she'd again briefly effaced herself in his presence and she wondered if she were still somehow under his sway.

Immediately after the encounter, she wrote him a mock letter over which she and Amelia shared a good laugh, but a day later Daria cringed at its melodrama.

In the weeks that followed, she found herself thinking about Ben's son, whose birth had occasioned their final conversation. "Don't you want to see little Ben?" he'd asked, then, a question she'd met with silence. "No, I guess not," he'd muttered finally, and hung up.

Now she pictured this teenager walking the streets of Manhattan, and she wondered if their paths might not even at some point have crossed. She imagined the revelation in store for him -- that behind closed doors his father was getting sexual favors from his patients, and she thought that, like her, he'd one day be felled by the truth.

She, herself, had only gradually realized the narrowness of her escape when Ben had re-married – choosing, in the end, a woman she'd initially envied but had come finally to pity. Still, over the years, the contours of Ben's face had constantly eluded her, so that she could never quite remember what he looked like -- as if he'd been a mirage. Now, too, having just seen him, she could bring him only vaguely to mind.

But she did recall his startling appearance on one long ago occasion. They'd been dining out, and he'd returned from the men's room with his wet hair slicked back. This flattened hairdo, combined with his greasy mouth and the dark stubble on his swarthy complexion had made him look shady, thuggish, and she'd been shocked at the sight of him, as if a screen had dropped from her eyes.

She'd fleetingly seen him this way the first time he'd tried to kiss her -- as old -- disreputable, but she'd dismissed this impression. Over time, she'd come to find him attractive, even irresistible, and at their recent meeting she'd also thought him good looking. But it was not his appearance that had drawn her again into his orb, she knew; it was rather an uncanny intimacy between them – a sense that she'd known him all her life.

In truth, Ben *was* disturbingly like her father, she thought, though the two men were also utterly dissimilar. The former was dark and husky, the latter fair and wiry. One was a doctor, the other a laborer. And while Ivan acted the clown, Ben was brooding, seductive. What her father and former lover did share, however, she concluded, was a charm that cloaked their true, predatory nature.

In Ben's presence she'd always felt inundated, washed over by a great wave. In the same way, her father's extravagant manner had, for a long time, flooded her senses, so that living in his house, she'd felt perpetually under siege. And just as she'd found her father alternately good looking and repulsive, so, too, had she been both attracted to and repelled by Ben.

It occurred to her, then, that her difficulty in visualizing Ben in years past stemmed from the same resistance to truth that accounted for her long years of blindness to the facts about her father. How parent like Ben had initially seemed -- helping her escape Marvin, supporting her through the break up and divorce, consoling and advising her. So that she'd come, finally, to regard him as her savior. But the precise nature of her relationship with him, she thought now, had always seemed murky, freighted with doubts, just as it had with her father.

As her therapist, Ben had drawn her into a physical intimacy which always fell short of consummation. When he'd pronounced her cured after the collapse of her marriage, she'd been stunned. But his assurances of ongoing friendship, she'd understood, constituted an implicit set up for an affair. From then on, and for years to come, she'd been at the mercy of his whims – reeled in at one moment, thrown out to sea the next, so that she was in a constant state of anguish and suspense.

It was Dr. Freid who'd opened her eyes to Ben's deviousness, his wolfishness. But even at the end, after Ben had re-married, she couldn't bring herself to hang up on his occasional phone calls, feeling somehow powerless at the sound of his voice, as if she could not fully escape his hold on her.

She realized with a shock, that only now, almost twenty years after their last contact, was she finally able to see Ben as the unsavory character he was. But to what else in her life, she wondered now, was she still blinded?

CHAPTER EIGHT

W hen Bronya decided to put her house up for sale, Daria was momentarily caught up in the mainstream of life. Absorbed with mundane concerns -- brokers, attorneys, money, she felt tenuously optimistic. Her mother's house, which represented her parents' highest strivings, had been for her a kind of inferno, and the prospect of its disposal stirred in her a revival of hope.

Bronya's search for an apartment briefly brought the sisters together. For the first time in years they conversed regularly, their conversations tinged, not with rancor, but anticipation, as if the relinquishment of the family home, a place steeped in dark memories, signified a new turn in their relationship.

Daria undertook the task of helping her mother hunt for an apartment. Recently retired, she'd hoped to spare her still employed sister the ordeal, to make up once again, for past negligence. But like one determined not to be outdone, Mimi also threw herself into the search. In the end, however, Bronya succeeded on her own, locating her new home through a friend.

She sold her house with equal pluck and independence, selecting a broker from among her acquaintances, then fixing on an inflated price, from which none of Jake's arguments could dissuade her. "She'll never sell it at that rate," he declared. But not only did she get her money, she got it more quickly than anyone had imagined possible, so that before they were quite ready for the change, Bronya found herself obligated to leave the home in which she'd lived for more than thirty-five years.

During this period of rapid change, Bronya demonstrated a resourcefulness so much at odds with her normal inertia, that for a brief interval Daria could only marvel at her mother's prowess.

Admiration, however, quickly turned to dread when it seemed as if Bronya might have to leave her house before she could take possession of her apartment. Daria advised her to stall the buyers, delay leaving one home until she could move into the other. When Bronya obstinately refused this advice, Daria foresaw the possibility of having to temporarily house her mother, a prospect at which she shuddered.

Driven now into a trap of her own making, she began to question her entire course of conduct. What *did* an adult child owe to a parent who'd consistently mistreated her, she wondered. In caring for her elderly mother she'd wanted only to do the right thing, but now she found the path to moral correctness becoming increasingly murky. Her mother's illness, her relative poverty, her difficulties with every day chores, her isolation -- the obligation to relieve these hardships was self-evident.

Yet now, as her mother's demands continued to increase while her own hopes for empathy dwindled, Daria's resentment gnawed at her, as if she were still a child in servitude to her parent. But, for the moment, she could see no way out. Bronya needed constant advice, constant reassurance. "Call the board members. Get early approval so you can move in on time," Daria urged -- counsel which finally brought the desired results.

But as soon as one problem was solved another surfaced. Her old friend attorney, whom Bronya obstinately refused to replace, turned out to be a slightly senile man in his nineties who'd so botched up the paper work that Daria, obliged to rectify the situation, began thinking about how to protect herself from her mother.

When Bronya said, "You'll help me with the packing," less a question than a statement, Daria said, "No. But I'll give you money to hire people who will." An answer Bronya disliked but was forced to accept. There was no escaping closing day, however, which entailed driving Bronya and her attorney to a distant, difficult to locate Long Island address while the two old people kept up a steady flow of complaints from the back seat.

Seated, finally, at the conference table with all concerned parties, Bronya immediately began to grumble in a variety of languages. Convinced she was being swindled, she continually jumped from her seat, prepared to launch into some tirade, while Daria pulled her down with whispered words of reassurance.

Moving day itself proved to be even more harrowing. While the morning went smoothly, with the house almost emptied by the time Daria arrived, the afternoon turned into a prolonged ordeal. Surrounded by unopened cartons crowded into a small space, Bronya, overwhelmed and fatigued, lost all her composure. Every difficulty elicited outbreaks of emotion. "Where's my wallet?' she shrieked at one point. "Oh my god, in all this commotion I lost my wallet. What will be? What will be?" she moaned, her face enflamed.

Daria placated Bronya's hysterics as she unpacked. With household help due to arrive in the morning, she'd hoped to get away by early evening. But even after she'd made the bed, unpacked necessities, shopped for groceries, brought in a meal, Bronya found yet another reason to keep her. And just as Daria was heading, finally, out the door, Bronya screamed, "Look what happened to my foot," which was, indeed, badly swollen. "What will I do? Who can find a doctor now? This will be the end of me," she wailed, while Daria rummaged for a basin.

She arrived home that night in a state of despair, recalling now the years of estrangement from Bronya as a welcome period of respite. What had possessed her to harness herself once more to her mother, she asked herself now. Why could she not free herself from her parent's tyranny?

But while Daria wrestled with these questions, events conspired to pull her into an ever deeper involvement. For years she'd worried about her daughter's future, possible wedding, fearing that when the time came, she'd have few relatives to invite. When Hannah's engagement became a certainty, therefore, Daria's relief at having a family circle to call on negated all other considerations.

With Hannah still in the mid-west and her fiancée in California, the wedding planning itself became a complex juggling act into which Daria nervously threw herself. She and Jake had married at City Hall, with no guests in attendance. But for her daughter, Daria wanted no less than the extravagant affairs popular among Hannah's friends, and she was grateful to have her mother and sister on hand for the occasion.

In the coming year, as Daria's grievances took a back seat to the nuptial festivities, she could almost believe she'd made some permanent peace with things as they were. And for Hannah's sake, she was so delighted with the show of relatives at the engagement party she could forgive Bronya her odd aloofness. This joyous event, Daria had imagined, would elicit from her mother a modicum of warmth, of approval. Instead, Bronya appeared detached, solemn, as if she were either harboring some secret grudge or could simply not be moved by the hoopla around her.

At the smaller, more intimate bridal shower, Bronya was more convivial, but here, too, she seemed unaffected by the elegant little soiree, like one accustomed to splendor. She displayed a similar smugness when she was being fitted for a wedding outfit, as if shopping at a couture salon were, for her, merely routine. She carped about everything, had to be cajoled, finally, into selecting a dress, and on the way out pointed longingly to other outfits she needed.

Nevertheless, relieved to be surrounded by family, Daria smiled at her mother with genuine warmth. "For the first time in my life I feel as if my daughter doesn't hate me," Bronya observed later to Mimi. The sisters shared a hearty laugh at this remark, marveling again at their mother's nonchalance, as if neither censure nor praise could penetrate her essential detachment.

At the wedding itself, Daria was too occupied to take much notice of her mother. But when they all posed for a group portrait, she impulsively took Bronya's hand, so that in the photograph, the smiling people surrounding the two women seated in the center with interlocking fingers had the look of a harmonious family.

Later, Daria was struck by this photograph's deceptiveness. With the wedding jubilation worn off, she could hardly account for her urge to take her mother's hand, except that she'd momentarily retreated into fantasy. The festivities at an end, Bronya's self absorption was again thrown into high relief. Every conversation became a listing of ailments. "In the morning everything hurts," she routinely complained. When not harping on her bodily functions, she gossiped about her acquaintances and neighbors, supplying detailed accounts of their lives and circumstances. Daria only half listened, responding with little more than an occasional grunt.

Seven years had now passed since she and her mother had

reconciled, and still there'd been no conversation about the past. No reckoning. No catharsis. No closure. During this time Bronya had continued to resist all mention of Ivan's offenses with such vehemence, that Daria had become resigned to her mother's indifference. When she and Jake decided to join Hannah in California, therefore, she rejoiced, thankful for the combination of circumstances that had made such a move both possible and desirable.

Keeping up the relationship with her mother all these years had worn her down, made her angry, resentful. She looked forward, then, to the relief of distance.

Mimi greeted the news of Daria's upcoming departure with surprising equanimity. Did her sister's restrained response signify a revival of filial affection, perhaps even remorse, Daria wondered. Was it possible that Mimi, moved finally, by her sister's suffering in the past, did not now begrudge her a measure of freedom in the future?

This was the hopeful picture Daria had drawn for herself. But while Mimi never carped about Daria's upcoming move, her tone became more acerbic. "If she gives me any trouble, I'm shipping her out to you," she sometimes remarked with a harsh laugh.

"Well. Who knows? Maybe..." Daria could only mumble.

Except for her occasional sharpness, however, Mimi appeared so sanguine about being left alone with their mother, Daria began to wonder why. She recalled Mimi's repeated refrain from years earlier: "We were just fine without you," and thought perhaps now, too, her sister preferred having Bronya, however difficult, to herself. Why, after all, Daria asked herself, *had* they been so fine without her? At the time, she'd attributed Mimi's stinging remark to the heat of the moment. But now, years later, she began to contemplate the awful possibility that Mimi had in fact, preferred a life long estrangement. Was this the real reason, then, for Mimi's composure in the face of their imminent separation? Did she, in fact, want to be rid of her sister so that she could the more easily maintain the fiction of a respectable family life – a fiction that had been carefully cultivated over all the years of Mimi's marriage?

She and Steven belonged to the same synagogue in which both sets of parents had been prominent members, and where a plaque honoring Ivan still hung. This was an appearance of respectability, Daria thought, which Mimi would want at all costs to preserve. And with her sister gone all threats to Mimi's fabricated reality would be removed. Besides, Mimi often reported exchanges with friends about the care of elderly parents with such relish that she appeared to enjoy her role as caretaker.

As she prepared for the much anticipated move to the west coast, however, Daria thought only peripherally about her sister. Relieved at Mimi's willingness to assume the burden of their mother, she tried to reconcile herself to her seemingly inexorable loneliness, to find consolation in the mild thawing of Mimi's habitual coldness toward her. "I had it easier growing up because I had you as a buffer," she'd commented once out of the blue, and whenever she and Jake appeared at their sons' various celebrations she'd always been effusively grateful.

Nevertheless, Daria embarked on her new life relieved to have left her relatives behind.

CHAPTER NINE

The snows came early the year Daria and Jake moved out west, so that by mid November, a month after their arrival, the Sierra Nevada Mountains were blanketed in white. And as they skied across the wide expanse of open meadow, the sky a vivid blue, Daria wondered if it were possible, even at her late stage of life, to re-fashion herself, to throw off the shackles of her sullied girlhood and enter the world anew. Here, surrounded by imposing peaks, limitless blueness and abundant sunlight, every kind of re-invention seemed within reach.

The agitations of her former life reverberated still, but their clamor had begun to fade. Whether she stood on the mountain peak or looked out over the deep waters of the lake, Daria felt the smallness of her own struggles, and she longed, then, to rid her mind of toxic influences. At this great distance her relatives were distant figures who had, after all, failed to love her. And ten years of renewed association with them had only deepened her wounds.

She would repudiate their hold on her, she told herself, give up her hopes and see them as they were. Even as a youngster she'd sensed the false center of her small universe, understood that her mother and father were not the people they pretended to be. As survivors of war they'd taken pride in their own courage and resilience. And to the world at large they'd appeared admirable, even heroic. Ivan had always claimed he was "strong like bull," and that nothing could kill him. Bronya credited herself with saving not only her own life during the war, but also the lives of those friends who'd fled with her to Siberia.

Bronya had also extolled herself as a mother, repeatedly telling the story of her illness following Daria's birth. The nurses, she used to say, had urged her to remain in their care. But because it was war time and the hospital was overcrowded, the infant, they'd said, would have to go. "You're young. You'll have more children." they'd told her. But despite her infection and high fever, Bronya had returned home with her baby, thus saving its life.

Bronya also pointed to her children's robustness as evidence of her good parenting. Whereas few Jewish children had survived famine in Siberia, her child, Bronya maintained, had thrived. Mimi, born three years later in a German displaced persons' camp, had also flourished, thus making both her children, Bronya liked to boast, the envy of other mothers.

Bronya also prided herself on having secured a free college education for her daughters. "You see how smart your mother is," she often said. "When I heard about this university in New York City for no money, I knew from this city I do not move."

Ivan, too, often pronounced himself an exemplary parent. "For whom do I work like a dog? For whom do I carry heavy shingles on my back," he liked to ask. "Everything I do, I do for you, for your sister," he often told Daria, tears moistening his eyes.

In thinking about her parents' claims of virtue, Daria had to concede the truth of their assertions. She and Mimi *had* survived the years of post war displacement in relative good health. And if not for her mother's prescience, she and her sister might, indeed, not have attended college.

Her father, too, Daria knew, had been the hard working, reliable family man he claimed to be. In the early days, when they were living in poverty, he liked to point out that, unlike his construction worker cronies, he never spent his money on drink but brought his entire pay check home to his wife, allowing himself few luxuries. And despite his limited English, his lack of education or skills, he'd persevered and done well in America, buying his own home, educating his children, providing his family with a decent life. These were accomplishments about which he often bragged. "How do you like your father the capitalist," he'd exclaim. "If a man like me, without a trade, without learning, can come here and make a living, then it is indeed good in America," he often said.

And Bronya agreed that America was, in fact, the "golden land." What she could never understand, however, was her elder daughter's obstinate refusal to smile. "Did you ever see such a child," she used to say. "A child who never smiles?"

As a youngster, Daria, too, was perplexed by her own gloom. But as she matured she began to find fault with her parents. She saw her father's swagger, his buffoonery, his coarse, excessive laughter and knew he was not quite like other parents. At the parties of her parents' immigrant friends, she noticed his too bright eyes, his flushed face, his unnatural exuberance, while she saw her mother dancing in the arms of other men, or talking to them with a rapturous expression.

She observed the way her parents flaunted themselves at these affairs, wearing finery beyond their means, demanding their daughters smile and talk prettily for their friends. But while

Mimi always complied, Daria would only frown and walk away. She sensed some secret affliction in the center of her family's life, some hidden disorder which marked and separated them, and this perception set her apart, made her feel that she didn't belong to them.

It was only in mid life, after years of therapy that Daria admitted to not only resenting her father, but her mother and sister, as well. Even then, however, she'd excused them as victims of Ivan's bullying, confident they three would reconcile after his death. But with Ivan gone for over twelve years now, and the past still unexamined and unlamented, Daria began to see her family's coldness as permanent, unassailable.

Living far away from them, she marveled at her self deluding suppositions. How, she wondered, could she have assumed that the woman who'd turned her back on her even in earliest childhood would become suddenly sympathetic? How, too, could she have believed that the sister whom she'd observed becoming increasingly hard as she matured would all at once be warm, compassionate?

Even as a child, Mimi, Bronya used to say, was "so selfish, she wouldn't give you a piece of ice in the winter." When they were children, and Daria had to mind her younger sister, as she often did, Mimi was invariably unruly, taunting. It was not until their adolescence, however, that Daria first began to recognize the depth of Mimi's antagonism toward her. Finding her weeping alone on the occasion of her teenage wedding, Daria had approached her sister with outstretched arms only to be rebuffed with such fury that she'd fled in tears. "Get away from me. I hate you," the then fifteen year old Mimi had shouted.

Over the years, when their divergent paths had occasionally crossed, Daria noticed an increasing harshness in Mimi's temperament, a coarsening of her language and a spitefulness in her moods which often made her wince. And whenever Mimi's sharp tongue was directed at her, Daria would freeze and feel alarmed -- not for herself, but for the little sister she saw hardening before her eyes.

But there'd also been moments of empathy between them, times when the anguish of their family life had thrown them weeping into one another's arms. In adolescence, they'd sometimes attended the theater together or found other common interests. And as young women, they'd even traveled through Europe in one another's company.

It was these memories of Mimi which had always fueled Daria's confidence in their intrinsic bond. Now, however, she began to question her own assumptions, to wonder if she and Mimi had ever really been friends. She thought about Mimi's letters, those written before and after Ivan's death, and for the first time she began to consider that Mimi's harsh, unpitying words reflected not passing emotions, but her abiding, unrelenting nature, a nature that seemed more and more to resemble that of their mother. Daria despaired at the idea of Mimi's growing likeness to Bronya, but at the same time she was glad of her own escape from the family's poisonous culture.

She recalled her mother's ongoing warfare with *her* younger sister, Chana, the battles so bitter that Daria suspected some buried family wound lay at the bottom of their combativeness. From hints and overheard remarks, Daria gathered that while Bronya often felt ill treated by Chana, Chana harbored a deep, permanent resentment toward her sister -- a resentment whose source only they two knew.

As a girl, Daria had scorned her mother's and aunt's hostilities toward one another, vowing never to duplicate their example.

But now she saw history repeating itself in her relationship with Mimi. Was this repetition only a coincidence, Daria wondered, or had the discord in the younger generation laid the groundwork for conflict in the older one? Daria had always heard from both her mother and aunt that Bronya had been her father's favorite, had had many admirers in her youth and was considered a great beauty in her home town. "She was always jealous of me," Bronya used to say about Chana, her face darkening with fury. But Daria had thought this an inadequate explanation for the depth of malice between the sisters.

She suspected, rather, that they each harbored some family secret which, if revealed might shed light on her own childhood suffering as well. Perhaps Bronya, too, had been molested in her youth, she thought, a possibility suggested by her years of blindness to her husband's pedophilia. Was it possible, in fact, that incest was not altogether uncommon among the large, impoverished Jewish families living in East Europe before the war, she wondered.

Even as a youngster, Daria had disliked her mother's landsmen. She invariably shrank from their too searching gaze and the strange mockery in their tone. They seemed always to be sizing her up, laughing at her. One woman, she recalled, used to regard her with a stern, knowing look, as if she'd sinned and been found out. In truth, Daria realized later, these landsmen were constantly taking one another's measure. "Do you know how much so and so must make," was a question often whispered among them. And while they all eagerly attended one another's celebrations, affairs intended primarily as displays of wealth, they rarely reached out to each other in times of need.

In fact, far from sharing her troubles with her friends, Bronya always sought to hide her worries from them. "No one must know. Tell no one," was her constant refrain at home. And the very people with whom she was most friendly in public were the same ones she often scorned in private, a practice, Daria guessed, of which they were all culpable.

The relationships among the landsmen were, in fact, marked by distrust, envy and malice. Bronya herself was in the habit of classifying her Jewish brethren as either "prousteh menschen," (common people) or "bessereh menschen," (refined people), and had always maintained that the "bessereh menschen," those with scruples and conscience, had, for the most part, not survived the war. And the fact was, all her mother's landsmen had always struck Daria as mean spirited, insincere and devious. Theirs was a culture full of concealment and innuendo. A culture in which unsavory truths were kept hidden and the appearance of prosperity was valued above all else.

Looking back at these people from her mountain perch, Daria was keenly conscious of her own escape from their unwholesome milieu – a milieu in which the children could be no less nasty than the adults. Daria remembered how her cousin Natalie, two years her senior, used to ridicule and trick her when they were girls, appearing then to relish the misery she'd inflicted. She recalled, too, how the teenage son of one landsman used to whisper smutty words in her ear then snicker as her eyes widened in alarm. And worst of all, she recalled Mimi's persistent, inexplicable malice toward her throughout their lives.

Within her own family, then, as well as among her parents' friends, Daria had always felt like a misfit. For the most part, the landsmen had taken little notice of her, only remarking repeatedly on her uncanny resemblance to Ivan. "Just look at her. She's an exact copy of her father," they'd exclaim in a tone which had always made her cringe. Later, she understood that Ivan, with his rough manners and Russian origins, was held in contempt by these more educated Polish Jews. But she could never be certain whether they disliked *her* simply because she so much resembled her father or because they sensed some indefinable taint about her person from which they shrank.

In her youth, Daria had endured her mother's landsmen by withdrawing from them, choosing as she got older to stay home alone rather than attending their events. But only in adulthood did she begin to understand that it was precisely because she'd rejected her parents' community that she'd avoided becoming like them. While Mimi always played happily with the few other refugee children, Daria kept to herself, becoming with each passing year increasingly critical of her environment.

As a youngster, she'd always been moved by the sight of the survivors condoling with one another over their war time suffering. And her spirits rose when they burst sometimes into Yiddish stories and songs, heartfelt performances which always blazed with emotion. As time went on, however, she saw the refugees becoming increasingly unfeeling and materialistic, more interested in showing off their wealth than in commiserating with their mutual hardships.

Having grown up within this ghettoized community, Daria wondered how she'd managed to escape. Had she risen above her environment precisely because of her suffering, she thought. Isolated by a dark, unfathomable affliction to which she could give no utterance, she'd always stood apart from her world, regarding the people in it with a detached, critical eye. Early on she'd begun to despise the materialism and insincerity of her parents' friends, and in her youth she'd vowed to be nothing like them, reserving her deepest disdain for her own mother. Where Bronya was cold and egotistical, she became effusive and self effacing. And where her mother was calculating and shrewd, Daria remained artless and naive.

This willful innocence had frequently worked against her, however, left her defenseless, vulnerable to exploitation. Even in her maturity her guilelessness led her sometimes into awkward entanglements, while her earnestness tended to arouse suspicion, animosity. In writing groups, too, her confessional stories had often been met with derision and disbelief. A few thought her tone was heavy handed. Some found her thinly disguised persona unsympathetic, even culpable. Others said the incidents of abuse were hard to believe. "That couldn't have happened," they said. Or, "That's not the way she would've felt."

Daria concluded then that the world at large was as averse to hearing about predatory fathers as was her own family, and she felt increasingly alone. But the need to tell her story continued to consume her. Her blighted childhood, her desperate youth, these polluted her mind. And the sense of mission that had taken hold of her in one decisive moment at age twelve still drove her.

She'd never forgotten that summer's day in the country. She'd been looking out into the horizon when she'd been struck suddenly by a sense of life's fraudulence – a conviction that beneath the benign surface of the ordinary lay darkness and danger. And as she'd stared into the distance, she'd felt a stirring, a call, as if the future were beckoning her, and for a moment, a vague image of the adult she'd inevitably become had taken shape before her eyes. Suddenly, she'd understood -- one day she, too, would be grown up. She'd have a voice. And when that time came, she vowed, she would speak; she'd tell the world about the inexpressible sorrow in its midst.

CHAPTER TEN

The ladies of the sisterhood crowded around her. When had she arrived? Why here? Why now? Her accent amused them. So blatantly New York. Quickly, she was one of them, many East Coast transplants like herself, several even from her old, Bronx neighborhood.

In the clean mountain air Daria felt a stir, an excitement. She let herself be carried off by the women, thinking vaguely some good might come of it. Seated with them around a table filled with food she basked in their warmth. "I love this group," one woman remarked. Their literary discussion had led to an exchange about marriage, fidelity and divorce, followed by personal revelations. Daria beamed, glad she'd taken on their book club.

But Jake objected. "Why are you getting so involved," he said. And at bottom Daria, too, sensed her efforts would come to grief. Yet even as the women of the congregation became tedious, she persisted – engaged now in her final dialogue with the world.

Every conversation with Bronya was nearly identical; she complained about her bowels, her morning aches, her weak heart. "I see," Daria said, or "uh huh," sometimes offering advice. "Drink a glass of hot water in the morning," or "take Metamucil."

She always hung up feeling doomed. But the distance between them, she persuaded herself, made their conversations bearable. Bronya would visit them once a year, she told Jake. "Because she's my mother," she shouted at him.

Having insisted on a wheelchair, Bronya emerged from the plane with a steward in attendance. At home, she sat groaning, "Oi vay. "Oy gevalt," as Daria unpacked her bags in a fever. She and Jake referred to her as the spider lady -- always watching, brooding, expecting -- mouth pursed, eyes narrowed.

In the car with Bronya, Daria shouted, "Shut your eyes," relegating her, finally, to the back seat, where she gasped in terror over the "windey" roads.

Good must come to good, Daria mused, sweeping Bronya in her wake as she entangled herself more and more with the women. "I present my mother, a holocaust survivor and self taught scholar of Jewish affairs," she announced at the sisterhood luncheon. Bronya, who'd parlayed her penchant for holding forth on all things Jewish into a role of amateur lecturer, regarded the audience somberly. Daria sat rigidly smiling, dreading the misconception she'd just unleashed. "On Sept. 1, 1939," Bronya began in her oracular voice.

"They all know this," Daria had shouted days before as the two of them sat hunched over the keyboard. "Tell them about *your* experiences," she'd urged. But Bronya, accustomed to speaking to her landsmen, who applauded anything she said, held fast. "They must be told," she insisted, as if she were the prophet come down from the mountain to deliver the news.

But she'd agreed, finally, to relate her own history too, electrifying the audience with her tale. Afterwards, people crowded around her; they wanted to talk to her, to shake her hand, to see her up close, to touch her. The following day a group took her out to lunch, and before she left they held a dinner in her honor.

At the next book club meeting one woman even quoted her. "We all have to live together," isn't that what your mother said, the woman asked, turning hopefully to Daria, her benign expression turning to fright at the unexpected response.

"My mother's the most racist person I know," Daria exploded. She'd arrived at the meeting intending merely to chip at the image she'd helped create. But hearing Bronya quoted inflamed her. "You of all people should know the dangers of bigotry, my daughter's always telling her," Daria declared in a kind of frenzy. Everyone sat frozen, eyes averted.

∽∾

Nights, Daria lay awake composing letters to Dr. Freid. "Dear Dr. Freid: More than five years have passed since we last met, at which time we parted with angry feelings on both sides. I'm writing to you now because...." Over the years, that opening had remained constant. The rest continued to vary: "During this time I've felt more and more troubled by your hostility toward me," she'd think. Or: "You did so much for in my youth that I am the more bewildered by your later antagonism."

❦

She offered her gifts to the women, scattering books on the table, devising lists, making up questions, composing summaries. Most seemed charmed, grateful. But others grumbled, resenting her presumption.

The crisis, when it came, was prompted by an unforeseen source. "I've just self published," Daria announced one day, and held up her book. She watched it move around the circle, her mind's eye holding the well known blurb: "A classic tale of immigrant struggle and success, as well as its antithesis: family dysfunction and child sexual abuse." As the women scanned the words, she observed their scowls, their lowered gaze, their silence. "I don't believe you," one woman declared, but nothing further was said.

When Daria mentioned her novel at the next meeting, one unwitting woman suggested they "do it," and another volunteered to lead the discussion. Warmed by this unexpected development, Daria felt vindicated. Good had, after all come to good she thought. "The club's going to do my book," she announced to Jake, who only regarded her with his usual impassivity.

❦

On the slopes, lulled by snow and sky, Daria felt the past recede. When she imagined Ivan's ghostly head watching her from above she felt mildly triumphant. But on flat ground the clamorous child drove her from the house. Turning her face to snow and wind, she trudged uphill to stare at the peaks and wait for enlightenment. In dry weather, looking out at the lake, she imagined sinking into its icy depths. On the bicycle, pedaling hard, watching for cracks and stones, she found respite. But at all hours she was pulled back -- as if advancing age acted not to dim memory but to deepen it.

∽◡◠

"You're very brave." Amelia remarked when she heard about the upcoming discussion of Daria's novel.

Inklings of trouble came when first one woman, then another asked her to withdraw her book. "Because no one wants to talk about this topic," they said

"If I do that I'll drop out of the sisterhood," Daria responded. Startled, they retreated.

The morning of the event there were frantic phone calls. "You mean you didn't arrange for rides?" Marlene, a purported friend, scolded. Daria made frenzied arrangements and girded herself for the thirty mile drive on the mountain road. She arrived in a state of high alertness, prepared for battle.

Inside, she gingerly approached the group gathered around a table heaped with food, avoiding their gaze as they avoided hers. The size of the crowd surprised her; she'd expected a sparse showing. They'd come to see her squirm, she guessed. Still, she hoped.

Briefly, the discussion did focus on the book itself, but one woman protested, "I don't want to hear these things about my, uh, friend," she said. Another veered the talk away from the book altogether. In the end, Daria likened the meeting to jumping into a tank full of sharks.

"That Ellen is a real bitch," Marlene said on the drive home, which set Daria off. "People are heartless, beastly. The most pernicious little vermin on the face of the earth, Jonathan Swift called them," she declared hotly.

She arrived home agitated and flushed. "They made mince meat out of me," she threw out at Jake, seated in his office.

"What did you expect?" he mumbled to his computer.

Seated in the den, looking out at the wide grassy yard from the wall to wall windows, Daria recalled lines she'd written some thirty years before: "There was that long year of my childhood/ A lonely time/ And I will live in a green house/ Surrounded by flowers." Odd that she'd been so prescient, she thought. Yet, here she was, well into middle-age, steeped in abundance. Shouldn't she discard the past, then, and move on, as the jargon of the day demanded, she asked herself.

Outdoors, large blue jays perched to drink from the yard's massive fountain. Watching them, Daria thought of the symbolic dropping of sins into waters by Jews on Yom Kippur, and she imagined doing the same -- depositing her memories into the lake and watching them float away. Or, she thought, if she could have herself bled, as people did in former times, she might rid herself of toxins. Instead, like the crazed mariner of the poem, she was driven to constantly re-tell her story.

Hearing the loud calls of the blue jays as they flew to and from the fountain, Daria envisioned the words of her book wafting like music through the air. Cheered by this image, she resolved to quit the sisterhood and go her own way.

※

"My book is in print," she wrote to Mimi, picturing her sister coming face to face at last with their father's crimes.

"Congratulations. Now you're a published author," Mimi wrote and nothing more.

Amelia said she loved the novel and sent her a lengthy comment, but with no mention of the key events.

Jake agreed to read it, but he never did.

Hannah thought the story should be widely read. But the note of hysteria in her daughter's voice gave Daria pause. In the past, she'd imagined intimate conversations with her adult child. Now she doubted one's offspring could ever be one's confidant.

Women begged her to teach them Shakespeare.

"It would mean a commitment," Daria hedged.

"Two, three sessions?" they asked.

"Two, three months," Daria said. The women gasped, but insisted they wanted to read HAMLET. Others joined in, so that five to eight of them were convening for weekly sessions in Daria's home.

"Why are you putting so much into this?" Jake asked. "Don't you see you're just the entertainment?"

Daria suspected he was right, but she couldn't give up a lingering hope.

"You make Shakespeare seem easy," they said, a remark from which Daria drew heart. In time, she thought vaguely....

Mimi announced she was coming to visit. She's just curious, Daria thought, but allowed herself a muted joy. Growing up, she'd been in awe of her popular, vivacious sibling, and as they matured, she'd wanted only to win Mimi's approval. Now, too, Daria hoped to impress her sister with her own sociability, as if a change in perception might engender intimacy.

For five days the two families lived in relative harmony. But at week's end Daria felt drained, dissatisfied. On the way to the airport Mimi talked non stop, with no reference to their time together, as if the visit had already been forgotten. At parting, she and Steven proffered nothing more than a simple thank you, which enraged Jake.

For months afterwards Daria saw herself being tossed from rock to rock. I don't like her, she thought of her sister. Yet, when Jake grumbled about Mimi's ingratitude, she countered, "I left her alone with my mother, didn't I?"

She called Bronya religiously -- even from abroad. "She's an elderly person living alone. I have to keep in touch," she said when Jake groused. But she knew her calls were fueled by some indecipherable compulsion.

"Why are you so good to your mother?" Amelia asked.

"To keep from killing her," Daria quipped, startled by her confession.

Their bi-annual visits to New York were marked by extravagance, so that even Bronya murmured, "This is too much," when Daria brought armloads of clothing to the cashier. For dinners, the family still gathered in their neighborhood Chinese restaurant, parting with heartfelt embraces. But at the final leave taking, when Bronya clung to her whimpering, Daria pushed her away -- shocking them both.

Back home Daria thought about time. She'd been thirty-nine when she'd recovered memories of her father's abuse; now she was fifty-six, too old, surely, she thought, to still feel tethered to her mother.

She took out Mimi's letters, which for years had lain hidden in a drawer. In each one she heard again her sister's enraged, pitiless voice. Poor Mimi, she used to think, certain they'd one day again be friends. As children they used to weep together, and in adolescence they sometimes helped one another. But in re-reading Mimi's letters today she wondered again if their friendship had ever existed.

"I do not want to hear anymore about what you uncovered in therapy. You have manipulated and sucked me into your unhappiness most of my life and I want no more of it! It's your problem, not mine." Mimi had written.

Dimly, Daria sensed a permanent rift coming, but she shuddered to think of it.

CHAPTER ELEVEN

A fter Bronya suffered another heart attack she was already
at Mimi's when Daria and Jake arrived. "If you don't get
her outta here I might kill her," Mimi said in greeting.

"Go do what you have to. I'll take care of things here," Daria
ordered, once more taking up the reins as the eldest.

Later, the four of them whispered urgently about finding help
for Bronya. "She doesn't want the Russians," Mimi screamed at
Steven, who retaliated, "She'll take what she can get."

"What about the Polish ladies she knows," Daria said, leaning
into their little circle.

"With my money your sister thinks she's a big shot," Jake
remarked later.

But Daria only regarded him absently.

"Better her than me," Mimi whispered to Daria the next
morning when the aid arrived, and they snickered together in
the old way.

For months afterwards Mimi called regularly with the same problem: her new, tyrannical boss. "The woman's a bitch," Daria agreed, always hoping to inject herself into the conversation. But before she could, Mimi changed jobs and her calls ended.

Listening to her mother's complaints, Daria wondered why she still felt beholden to her, why she was driven constantly to please her. "I can't stand to look at her sour puss every day," Bronya said of her care giver.

"I'm worried the two of them will kill each other in that small apartment," Mimi mocked.

∽∾

"When are you coming to New York?" Bronya always asked. But for two years Daria stayed away.

When she and Jake showed up again they'd just returned from Poland.

"You're going to Kalisz?" Mimi had marveled.

"Yes," Daria had only muttered, wishing she could say more. But the distance between them seemed too great.

"It was like a picture book," Bronya used to say about her home town. "Such trees! Such flowers! On Sundays everyone would dress up and stroll in the park. So beautiful it was. And the air was not polluted like it is here in this stinking city. There you could breathe." she'd say.

"Everywhere you went you were surrounded by family. Aunts, uncles, cousins, I had so many I couldn't count them all. Everyone knew everyone else. You were never alone, never afraid. And there was so much culture. We Jews had our own clubs, our own organizations, classes, groups, discussions, theater. You were never bored," she said, painting so idyllic a picture of Kalisz that

Daria had often longed to be there rather than her grimy Bronx neighborhood.

As a youngster she used to love hearing about her mother's lost home. Seated at the kitchen table while Bronya ironed, she'd listen to her tales of Kalisz and visualize herself there – strolling in the park, stopping by the stream, greeting friends and relatives. Her heart was naturally drawn to Kalisz. Here the grandparents she'd never known had lived and generations of her maternal family had been rooted.

For years, however, she'd resisted going, loath to embark on a journey ordinarily undertaken in homage to a beloved parent. But she realized, finally, she must go, not for her mother's sake but for her own.

Bronya was full of fears. "Do you know how anti-Semitic those Polacks are? You could get hurt. They're afraid the Jews are coming back to reclaim their properties," she said. When her qualms were pacified, however, Bronya was overcome by emotion. "What a wonderful thing you are doing, mameleh," she said in the coming months. So once again Daria found herself feeding the very pretense she wanted to dispel.

Kalisz itself, a place she'd so often conjured, seemed to Daria a kind of dreamscape, and she walked the streets in a trance. Everything looked oddly familiar, as if she'd lived here in some remote past. And only when she stood in the town square did she remember that she had, in fact, been here before -- for several months after the war. Then she'd been a mere eighteen months old, too young, surely, she thought, for memory. Yet, as she wandered the neighborhoods about which she'd heard so much she felt as if she'd come home.

Nor had her mother exaggerated the town's beauty. The historic square, with its antique, ornately carved, multicolored buildings spoke of a bygone era of elegance and grace -- as did the park, with its meandering stream and lush trees, the imposing theater, the grand boulevard and stately homes.

Her mother's family, however, had lived on the poorer side of town. And as Daria walked these streets and entered the now shabby buildings, she summoned them all: the mamashie with her angular face and stylish dress, the tatishee with his dandified air and roguish smile, the beautiful, youthful Bronya, the young, tom boyish Chana, the diligent brother Psachia, the affectionate, playful youngest, Zalek. They'd each stood on this spot, walked down this street, looked out at these sites, Daria thought as she conjured the spirits of the dead grandparents and murdered boys.

The small grocery which her great grandfather had owned was still an operating store that seemed little changed. Peering inside Daria could almost see her great grandmother, small, round and wearing the traditional "sheitel" (wig), standing behind the counter. When Daria stood in the hallway of the apartment building this family had owned, and in which many of them had lived, she could almost hear them shouting and bickering as of old.

They found Bronya's beloved school, the one to which she'd walked several miles each way when her family moved. "I was the best student there. All the teachers loved me. The day I graduated, when I was only fourteen years old, was the saddest day of my life," she used to say.

This building, a still operating elementary school was a neat, modest stone structure sporting a colorful emblem at the entrance honoring its name sake, the poet, Adama Mickiewicza. How often had Daria visualized her mother's long daily walks to and from her school and imagined her grief on graduation day. To be standing at last on this leafy, bucolic street, in front of the very building she'd often pictured, was to connect with a past that had for years lived only in her imagination.

Nowhere were the spirits of her lost relatives more palpable than in the town market place, now a supermarket. Here, the Jews of Kalisz had been rounded up for eventual transport, and it was from this site that Bronya and her sister had said their last farewell to their parents. "There were only two bathrooms for thousands of people," Bronya used to say, and as Daria looked out now at the ordinary scene: the stacked shelves, the shoppers with their carts, she tried to visualize the frightened hordes that had been jammed into this dank, cavernous building.

She pictured the tumult, the long lavatory lines, the restless crowds. She imagined nineteen year old Bronya taking final leave of her parents, her mother still beautiful in her brown suit, and she felt herself paying homage to those blood relatives she'd never met.

All over town there were vestiges of a vanished Jewish life: destroyed synagogues, apartment buildings that had once housed Jewish schools, former Jewish neighborhoods in which no Jews lived, the theater in which Yiddish plays were no longer performed. And Daria felt the teeming world of her mother's stories come to life.

Throughout her childhood, Kalisz had been for Daria a mythic place from which she'd been inexplicably excluded. The idyllic town, the fond relatives, the cultured life – these had always seemed to belong solely to her mother. And as she'd navigated her own brick and cement neighborhood, with constant moves from one outpost to another her only prior memory, she often felt rootless, flimsy -- as if the solid world of her parent did not pertain to her. In Kalisz itself, however, she imagined herself surrounded by the spirits of the generations of her family who'd lived here -- and their history, seemed, finally, to be part of her own.

≈

Back in New York, Daria's mind teemed with images of Kalisz. The streets and buildings her relatives had inhabited, the park they'd strolled, the square they'd frequented, the market place into which they'd been crowded, the school her mother had attended -- these sites appeared to her now as memories of a world to which she, too, could lay claim.

"Oh, mameleh, what a wonderful thing you have done," Bronya said when Daria arrived with videos of Kalisz.

But Daria could hardly keep from shouting, "This doesn't mean I love you."

≈

At home, she prepared a Kalisz album for her mother and marveled at her own perversity.

Mimi, in the meantime, wanted to withdraw funds from Bronya's account for a pre-paid funeral. "When she dies I'm not laying out fifteen thousand dollars to bury her," she declared hotly.

"Why would you have to?" Daria asked.

"If the state freezes her assets that's what'll happen," she insisted.

When Jake dissuaded her from this plan, Mimi proposed others. "What if she has to go into a nursing home? Do you have any idea how fast her money will be sucked up?" she said, laying out schemes for siphoning off Bronya's savings, each of which Jake systematically rejected.

Where had Mimi's mercenary bent come from, Daria wondered. As a hippie graduate student living on a California ashram her talk had always centered on money. "Bread," she used to call it, pronouncing the word with a bitter inflection. In her few letters home she'd constantly demanded fresh funds, which Ivan secretly granted, while Bronya, ever suspicious, groused. And once, Daria recalled, Mimi had accused their mother of stealing from her.

"Your sister can't stand the fact that you have more than her," Jake remarked.

"No one likes to be the poor relation," Daria said.

"They're hardly beggars," Jake countered.

Mimi began to call with alarming tales about their mother. She'd been seen coming in and out of the apartment at all hours of the night. Her microwave, she'd begun to insist, was dangerous, and her cleaning woman was stealing from her. "She's paranoid," Mimi said. "She keeps badgering me she'll die alone in the apartment and no one will know. But if she thinks she's moving in with me she's off her rocker. I got rid of all my extra beds. There's no room for her here," she shouted.

Yet, she, like Bronya, rejected assisted living. Both feared the cost and Bronya trembled at the change. "Do you have any idea how expensive it is?" Mimi gasped.

"Jake says she can afford it," Daria offered, but Mimi demurred.

"She doesn't want to spend her inheritance," Jake mocked.

Events finally took over, however, when, after a brief hospital stay, Bronya dreaded returning to her apartment alone. "Let's move her now, while she's still in transition," Daria urged, to which Mimi responded with startling alacrity.

"I've signed the lease. They can take her in two weeks," she announced days later.

Surprisingly docile, Bronya agreed to both the sale of her apartment and an interim nursing home stay. And as Mimi undertook all the necessary transactions, she called regularly with updates and questions. Should the place be painted? Should the kitchen counter be replaced? Should she sign with a broker, she asked. But she rejected Daria's offer of funds for professional packers. "Why? So they can steal from me?" she said.

"She can't wait to pick through your mother's things," Jake remarked dryly.

"But she's doing all the work," Daria countered.

With great difficulty, she reached Bronya daily on the single ward phone at the nursing home. But Mimi turned down her offer to fly out and help with the move.

"She doesn't want you to see what she's grabbing," Jake said.

"She can have it all," Daria snapped. "Isn't she putting the sale of the apartment in your hands," she said. But days after Jake had vetted brokers Mimi announced she'd handle the selling herself.

"You'd better warn her about those real estate sharks," Jake said.

Then Mimi went ahead and signed just the sort of contract about which she'd been alerted. "Why didn't you consult us?" Daria pleaded

"Stop treating me like a child. You think you know everything but you don't," Mimi replied.

"How long can I make you mother's savings last with two rents to pay? You'd better let her know what's going on," Jake insisted.

But Bronya only shouted, "Stop fighting over my money."

For months, her apartment remained unsold. "If your sister's such a big shot, let her support your mother when she's destitute," Jake complained.

"She'll just have to go on welfare," Daria declared, but she trembled at the idea – her mother impoverished while she lived in splendor. "Being in charge of all that money went to Mimi's head," she fumed, her view of her sister steadily darkening.

CHAPTER TWELVE

Eyes shut, Daria saw her mother and sister, their forlorn faces rising like emanations of her own grief. She left them in stages, beginning with her final visit.

"Ma. I told you a million times, don't keep money lying around," Mimi scolded, while Bronya sat with a blank, child like expression. "Are you listening?" Mimi said.

"All of a sudden she's like a two year old. She can't unlock the door. She can't dial the phone. She can't turn on the TV," Mimi whispered. But Daria had the impression she was enjoying herself.

"Do you have any idea how much paper work I had to do," Mimi went on. "Between the nursing home, Medicare, this place, her apartment, I've been swamped. But I set up a great filing system," she boasted.

Steven's expression, too, as he reclined on the cluttered sofa, seemed to Daria smug, disdainful. He called Bronya, "Ma," and talked to her with the slight impertinence of a son.

Surrounded by Mimi's family photographs in her mother's new, tiny apartment, Daria imagined her sister and brother-in-law taking charge of Bronya -- picking through her things -- arranging her rooms – directing her movements. And she sensed that the proprietary tone with which they spoke to Bronya was meant for her benefit.

At dinner that evening in an over crowded, noisy restaurant of Mimi's choosing, she bragged about her friend the attorney, the crowd they socialized with, the yacht party they attended – in all of which Daria felt a rebuke, a pushing away.

"Did you ever see him put his hand in his wallet?" Jake grumbled later about his brother-in-law.

∽∾

Seated the next morning amid Bronya's familiar squalor, Daria's sense of separateness from the family hit her with renewed force, and as the day went on she became increasingly agitated. At the shoe store, she shouted at Bronya, "What're you afraid of," almost lifting her bodily from the seat when she refused to stand up in her new shoes.

At dinner, she ran repeatedly to Bronya's side -- to wipe her chin, pick up her napkins, brush away crumbs. Nor was Jake spared Bronya's tyranny. When he remarked that the continued non sale of her apartment might mean a move into a nursing home, she shot back, "If you put me there I'll come back to haunt you."

"She's got balls, biting the hand that feeds her," Jake muttered later in disbelief.

∽∾

Daria spent the next morning preparing for luncheon with her nephew in their Manhattan hotel suite – an invitation Mimi had also condescended to accept. "Will you two join us for lunch, or would you prefer not to," Daria had offered, knowing her sister would feign indifference.

She and Steven came in with a studied nonchalance and sank into arm chairs like people accustomed to luxury, while Daria, unable to curb her feverish chatter, plied them with food and drink.

The family's parting that afternoon was, as always, rife with innuendo. While Jake maintained his usual aloofness, the group's banter as they approached the parking garage became increasingly high pitched, increasingly jovial. The car in sight, Daria detected the usual play of emotions on her sister's face: sadness followed by anger, followed by resignation. And she imagined Mimi's grievances: "I was there when dad died. Where were you? I was there when mom had her anxiety attacks. Where were you?"

Back home, Daria stood at the edge of the lake looking out over the panorama of water and mountains and thought about the treachery of time, its power to seduce one with the allure of the future – the unknown. She recalled herself some twenty years earlier, taking off the way she used to as a child. And just as she'd often run to a distant pond as a girl, she fled decades later to a far away bay, wondering as she gasped for air from what she was fleeing. But as she'd looked out over the narrow inlet, she heard only Dr. Freid's voice exhorting: "You hate men. You don't want a man in your life."

She'd searched her mind, then, for answers, but found only the familiar wall – the one against which she'd been beating her fists all her life. Yet, as she'd turned back toward home that day, she felt a shifting, a loosening, as if change might still be possible.

It was a short time later that she'd begun to tear down the inner barrier, to retrieve, finally, the memories hidden on the other side. She recalled the months when the revelations had come thick and fast, sending her spiraling into a place where the ground could no longer be relied upon to support her and where all her certainties were shattered. As each brick had given way, then, she'd looked back on the forty years behind her: the baffled childhood, the sordid adolescence, the anguished youth, and seen that all her life had been a search for just this knowledge, this recognition that had, in fact, always been at hand. And the years of blindness had seemed then like a long illness from which she'd recovered at last.

How elusive had been that hope of redemption, Daria mused now as she gazed out at the blue waters of the vast lake. Yet, hadn't she suspected all along that her family relations would ultimately disintegrate -- that in the end she'd be facing the old, familiar emptiness. "Enough!" a voice in her seemed to cry, as she thought back to all the years of trying to wring comfort from those fortified against her. And as she looked out now into the horizon, where snow covered mountains seemed to rise from the waters, she knew with a heart sickening certainty that nothing would ever pierce their armor.

But she couldn't leave them without a final advance. And when Bronya agreed to read her autobiography she even allowed herself a sliver of hope. "What a terrible thing," Bronya moaned when, after months of delay, she finished the book at last. "So this is what he was doing. This is what he was doing," she mumbled. "And I was so bad. I was so bad," she admitted. "I'm sorry," she said. "I didn't know. If I'd known I'd have killed him."

"So now will you tell Mimi I'm not crazy, that I'm not a liar, Daria urged, grabbing at this unexpected show of penitence.

But at this Bronya demurred, resorting under pressure to her customary threat: "If I die tonight it'll be your fault."

With Mimi, Daria proceeded more cautiously. "I'm not sparing her anymore," she said of their mother. "Because the older I get the more bitter I feel about what happened to me, not less." When this got no response, she wrote: "I've been having explosive conversations with Bronya, telling her it was she who turned you against me and she who has to fix it."

"I'm not her puppet. I was angry with you on my own. You just disappeared!" Mimi fired back.

"Let's finally deal with this family tragedy together," Daria responded.

To which Mimi replied, "Some people choose to live in the present!"

"What if he'd come after you instead of me? Could you then so easily dismiss the past?" Daria answered.

Days later, a New Year's card signed, "Lots of Love," arrived from Mimi in the mail.

"We cannot be a family without talking about Ivan and the way you all turned on me when I told you what he did to me," Daria wrote.

And then, silence.